MW01087553

Published January 2024
Published by Indies United Publishing House, LLC

Cover art by Leslie A. Piggott

ISBN: 978-1-64456-674-9 (paperback)
ISBN: 978-1-64456-676-3 (ePub)
ISBN: 978-1-64456-675-6 (Mobi)

Library of Congress Control Number: 2023948907

INDIES UNITED PUBLISHING HOUSE, LLC
P.O. BOX 3071
QUINCY, IL 62305-3071

www.indiesunited.net

The Mystery of Specter Island
The Cari Turnlyle Series: Book 4

by Leslie A. Piggott

INDIES UNITED PUBLISHING HOUSE, LLC

Dedication

To my forever-love: Brad, thanks for always planning the best trips

Chapter 1

Lydia sat up in her bed and looked around. Goosebumps covered her arms. Someone was downstairs; she was certain of it. She looked at her bedside clock: three a.m. All of her current guests were on the second and third floors. She kept the basement locked during the night. The TV and game rooms were down there and she had learned early on that keeping the area off limits during normal sleeping hours was best.

She heard a door slam and cringed. This was the third break-in in the last month. For the most part, she had managed to keep the news of the break-ins from the public, though, she felt obligated to report them to any current and future guests. During the second break-in, a man staying in a second-floor room heard a window break and beat her to the dining room. He helped her clean up the glass and, thankfully, hadn't immediately checked out.

Lydia tugged on her robe and grabbed her large ring of keys from her dresser. She unlocked the door to the stairwell and crept downstairs to assess the damage. She listened for any sounds from the upper levels that might indicate another guest had been alerted to the intruder, but the big house was silent.

The basement had three window wells on both its long sides and two more on one short side. She had recently begun replacing all of the windows, as one had been broken during the first break-in too. It had cost her more than she expected and she was relieved to see that all of the windows were still intact. She crossed the room to the exterior door. It was another emergency exit. You could go through it without a key from the inside, but it was always locked from the outside. She pressed the push bar on the heavy door and looked at the jam. It didn't take a forensic science degree to see that someone had used a crow bar to pry the door open. She took a quick peek at the area near the stairs that led up to the parking lot. She was pretty sure that whoever had broken in was long gone, but she wasn't planning on confronting the intruder. The concrete steps were deserted and besides the sounds of the wind blowing through the trees, the world around her was silent.

She sighed and stepped outside to see if the door still locked properly. The air was brisk and the wind whipped her grey hair into her face. She tucked it back behind her ears and pushed the door closed. She heard it click, which usually meant that it had locked. Just to make sure, she tried pulling the door open. It was locked tight. Lydia exhaled with relief. At least she didn't need to have the door repaired or replaced. She pulled out her master key and let herself back in.

Now to see what damage was done on the inside. She looked around the room and initially wondered if the break-in was some sort of hoax, something to scare her. Then she spotted the bookshelf. It held books of all genres as well as old guest books that dated back to the origination of the business. Grandfather Willoughby, her ancestor five generations back, had opened the bed and breakfast as a boarding house in the mid-1800s for the gold rushers to stay on their way to California. The guest books were scattered across the floor. Some of them had pages that had come loose, either from age or the carelessness with which they were discarded. She knelt down to pick them up and get them back on their shelf.

Normally, she would carefully put each of them back and make sure they were in chronological order, but it was three in the morning and she would rather get some more sleep. Her mind drifted to her nephew, Bob, who was due to arrive with his girlfriend in a few days and she wanted everything to be perfect for his stay. Bob was a forensic scientist of sorts and would be appalled that she was touching evidence in a possible crime without gloves. She frowned at this realization. Bob was coming for vacation, not work. She didn't want to bother him with her troubles. She slid the last volume into place and stood up. Time to get some shut-eye.

Chapter 2

C ari Turnlyle yawned and rubbed the sleep from her eyes. The sunlight was peeking through the curtains already. She hoped that meant the storms from the past few days were finally over. It had been dreary and wet for at least a week. She was ready for the sunshine.

Cari's job as an investigative journalist for the local newspaper, The Brenington Beagle, kept her busy. During the previous year, the normally quiet town in New York had seen a spike in crime. Cari had helped solve four murders and stop an arsonist on the loose in her city. Thankfully, the last six months had been relatively calm. The newspaper had hired a new journalist at the end of last year, alleviating her work load substantially. Bryson Millar had moved to the area from New Mexico, where he had worked for over twenty years as a journalist. He preferred the political aspect of the news and balanced Cari's journalism style well. They had found a nice rhythm of managing the local news and events together. Cari hadn't taken a vacation since starting with the Beagle almost five years ago and was ready for some time away.

Her boyfriend, Bob, had asked her if she could take off for a week to ten days so they could go on a trip together. She had never traveled with anyone except her family and was a little hesitant to say yes at first. Though she and Bob occasionally slept over at each other's apartments, they hadn't really discussed moving in together. Going on a vacation together seemed like a big step for their relationship. Bob suggested she request the time off first and then make up her mind about traveling with him. When Ollaman, the editor and her boss at the Beagle, said he would be happy for her to take a week off, she decided to go for it. She didn't know what Bob had planned for the trip. He had told her to pack swimwear, active wear, casual clothing, and something dressy for dinners out.

Bob had asked her to be ready to go by nine o'clock. She hadn't done any packing yet, but she still had over an hour. Once she got out of the shower, she could get everything in her suitcase. She swung her covers off and rolled out of bed. She needed to get the coffee machine going first; then she could shower. *Then* she could pack. She had barely reached her bedroom door when her phone started ringing with Bob's ringtone. She quickly grabbed it and answered while hurrying over to the coffeemaker.

"Hey, Bob! I was just about to jump in the shower. What's up?"

"Just checking in. Were you able to fit everything in one bag?"

Cari chewed on her lip and mentally debated her response. "Uh, one bag…"

"Have you packed anything yet?" He laughed.

"Well, I have thought about it a lot." She responded as she poured the coffee grounds into the filter and hit start.

"Okay, I'll let you get to it. Text me if you think you're going to need to check a bag."

"Ok, will do. See you soon."

"Love you, Cari."

She smiled. "Love you too."

She and Bob started dating a little over nine months ago. Bob had initiated the relationship. Cari had been a little uncertain about going from friends to dating; she didn't want to lose their friendship. He had won her over and she hadn't regretted it for a minute. Back in March, he confessed to her that he said "I love you" into the phone after she hung up and had been doing that for a few weeks, trying to work up his nerve to say it to her in person. She smiled as she remembered the conversation. Bob was the kindest person she knew; she didn't deserve to be loved by someone so great. She was grateful for his presence in her life.

The coffeemaker beeped, bringing her back to the present. She clapped her hands to try to propel herself into action. *Coffee, shower, pack, let's do this!*

Cari wrapped a towel around her head hoping to speed up the drying process and took another gulp of coffee. She realized that her good intentions of making a packing list the evening before had not come to fruition. She would just have to wing it as usual. She pulled open her dresser drawers and counted off seven of each item as she tossed them onto the bed. Laughing at herself, she stopped and decided to get her suitcase out before going any further.

She lifted the edge of the bedspread and peered under her bed. A few wayward socks lingered in the shadows, along with some charging cables and an empty water bottle. She sighed. She thought she had stuffed the suitcase under the bed after using it last. Maybe it was in the coat closet. Flipping the closet light switch on, she looked inside. One jacket hung on a hanger while two others seemed to have slipped off. They had fallen in a heap on the floor. She lifted them and breathed a sigh of relief. Her green suitcase sat on its side in the corner. She set the jackets aside and pulled the suitcase out.

She quickly unzipped it and then scooped all of the clothing from the bed inside. *That was easy enough!* She padded over to her bedroom closet and selected her favorite long cardigan to go along with a green-striped shirt and some jeans. She knew they were flying somewhere but wasn't sure how much walking they would have to do in the airport. She settled on her sneakers for footwear rather than her more stylish flats, just in case. She tossed the flats over to the suitcase on the bed. She mentally crossed items off of her packing list and decided she just needed to get her toiletries and she'd be ready to go.

She returned to the bathroom after tugging on her clothes. She had travel-sized toiletries in the bathroom drawer already in a bag. Thankfully, it held a set of makeup too, so she didn't need to gather any of the items from the countertop. She tried to brainstorm where they might be going as she finished getting ready. *Maybe a beach? He said to bring my swimsuit. Or maybe there's a pool at the hotel. Or maybe—*

Cari was just finishing applying her makeup when a knock at her door startled her as she was applying her mascara. She frowned and jumped up to answer the door. Before she could peek through the peephole, Bob called out to her.

"Cari, it's me! Are you ready?"

She unlocked the door and pulled it open. "Hey Bob, I'm just finishing one thing...what?"

"Trying out a new look today?" He crinkled his nose at her. He was dressed as usual in khaki pants and a polo shirt.

"Oh, what?" She scurried back to the bathroom to look in the mirror and laughed. "Well, this is definitely a new look!"

A long black line streaked across her face from the corner of her right eye to her hairline. She grabbed a tissue and used some water to wipe it off. She probably should have just gone without makeup. She usually only wore it for special occasions, but the trip seemed special.

"All set?" Bob asked from the living room.

"I think so. Let me just grab my bag," she said as she walked over to her bed. Cari grabbed the suitcase handle and began to pull it from the bed. Unfortunately, she had not zipped it closed, so everything flew out onto the floor. "Oh no!"

Bob ran over to see what was wrong. He sighed and then laughed. "Can I help you scoop everything back inside?"

Cari already had an armful and was tossing it into the bag again. "Sure. You know, now that I can see everything again, I think I forgot to pack dress clothes. Whoops!"

Eventually, she had everything in the bag and they were on their way to the airport. Cari's foot bounced in anticipation of the day. She was really curious to find out where they were going.

"So, when do I get to hear of our destination?"

Bob grinned. "Well, first, we have a flight to Minneapolis—"

"Minneapolis! I've never been there."

"Well, that's not our final destination. We're going to rent a car and drive a few hours into Wisconsin."

"Oh, I've never been there either. Will we get to see the Great Lakes?"

"We will get to see one Great Lake. Lake Superior. That's all I'm saying for now. I'll send you your boarding pass after we park."

Cari smiled. "I'm really excited, Bob. Thanks for planning a vacation for us."

* * * * *

The flight to Minneapolis was on time. After making their way through security, Cari got them both a coffee and a bottle of water while Bob found some snacks to tide them over until they could eat lunch. She sat down next to Bob at the gate and started rifling through her bag for the book she was reading. Bob was sending someone a text. He looked up when she sighed.

"Everything okay?"

She frowned. "I thought I packed the book I was reading, but I can't find it in here. I guess it's still in my apartment."

He bit back a grin, but she could see the humor in his blue eyes. "You? Misplace something?"

"Shut it. I might have packed a bit hastily."

"You could always buy a new book to read from one of the shops around here. If you don't mind the mark up, of course."

Cari smiled. "I have some e-books on my phone. I'll just read one of those. Hey! Let's take a selfie, document the start of our vacation!"

She took out her phone and opened her camera app. Bob leaned in and she did her best to fit them both into the frame before clicking the button. The image was a little crooked but satisfactory.

Bob's phone buzzed with an incoming text. He glanced at the screen, then turned the phone to silent and slid it into his pocket. Cari wondered who he was chatting with but figured he would let her know if it was important.

She had barely read a handful of chapters in her e-book when the gate attendant announced it was time to board their flight. It would take them a little over three hours to reach Minneapolis. She opened her boarding pass on her phone and stood up to wait with the rest of the travelers. Bob did the same. Before putting on his backpack, he unzipped one of the pockets part way, looked inside, and then quickly rezipped it. She gave him a funny look, but he didn't notice.

They got settled into their seats and watched as the plane filled with passengers. As they pushed back from the gate, Cari noticed Bob sending another text to someone before putting his phone in airplane mode. They didn't have to wait too long to be cleared for takeoff. Cari closed her eyes as she always felt a little uneasy during the start of a flight. She tried to think about something else to take her mind off of the bumps they were experiencing. *Bob has sure been on his phone a lot this morning. Usually, he hardly touches it. I wonder who he's been texting. Maybe it has something to do with the trip. I probably should have texted or called Grandmother. Oh well, I can do it when we land...*

"Cari! Look out the window!" Bob's voice startled her awake.

"Oh! I didn't realize that I fell asleep." She looked out the window and saw the Great Lakes below. "That's incredible. I've never seen them before. You said that we're going to be near Lake Superior?"

Bob nodded. "Yes. We have about a four-hour drive after we land. I hope that's okay."

"Of course! It will be great. A road trip and a spectacular view. Win-win."

Cari yawned and rolled her head from side to side. She wasn't usually one to nap and felt a little silly about falling asleep in the middle of the day. She looked at her watch and raised her eyebrows.

"Was I asleep for almost two hours?"

Bob looked at his own watch. "Thereabout, yes. I saved you some snacks. Are you hungry?"

"I am, thanks. What do you have?"

He handed her a bag of pretzels and a granola bar. "I have some candy too, if you want any of that."

"I'll keep you posted. We're still getting lunch after we land, right?"

"Definitely! We should be on the ground in about an hour."

"I completely forgot to call Grandmother before we took off," Cari told him.

"I wondered if you were thinking about her earlier. I saw you fingering your locket as we were taking off."

Cari blushed slightly. "You're right, I was thinking about her. I meant to tell her that we were headed to Minneapolis. I guess I can give her a better update once we land."

"I know she'll be excited to hear from you. Isn't she spending time with your sister and her kids this week?"

"Oh, that's right! Bea was going to bring the kids up after their school lets out for the summer. I think their last day was yesterday. Hilary and Joel were really excited about it. I know Grandmother loves getting to see them more." Cari smiled as she thought about her niece and nephew.

"How is Robby's job? I haven't heard her talk about it since they first moved in."

"I'm not sure. You're right; she doesn't mention it much. He seems really busy, though."

"I guess that's good, right?" Bob asked.

"Seems like it." Cari looked out the window again.

The plane bumped around a bit and she saw they were passing through some clouds. The fasten seatbelt sign illuminated and a flight attendant announced they would experience some turbulence for a few minutes and to please remain seated. Cari ate a few pretzels. The turbulence was fairly mild, but she hoped it would pass soon. She hadn't flown in years and had forgotten it kind of put her on edge when the flight wasn't smooth.

"What kind of food would you like to have for lunch?"

"Oh, I don't know. Not a sandwich."

Bob pretended to take notes. "No sandwiches. Okay, got it."

She laughed. "What sounds good to you? Have you been here before?"

"It's been a few years, so I'm not sure what's around. I thought we might get something light and then have more food at dinner."

"That works for me." She felt the plane drop a bit and realized they were in the initial descent just as the flight attendant made the announcement.

"I'm going to read a little of my book before we land. Do you want any more pretzels? I think I'll save the granola bar for later."

Bob took the bag of pretzels from her and returned them to his backpack. The man seated to Cari's right was asleep.

11

"Has our seatmate been asleep the whole time?" Cari asked, leaning over to Bob.

"I think so. He'll wake up when we land. It's nearly impossible to sleep through that."

Just as Bob predicted, the man jerked awake when the plane's wheels hit the runway. Cari looked in the seatback pocket just to double-check that she hadn't stuck something in there. Satisfied that it was free of her belongings, she pulled her messenger bag out from under the seat in front of her. When she turned to look at Bob, he was already sending a text on his phone. He looked her way and then slid the phone into his pocket.

"Everything okay?" She asked him.

"Huh? Oh, yeah. Everything is fine. I was, uh, just…checking in with Chris at work," he stammered a bit through his words.

She raised her eyebrows. "And?"

He gave her a blank look at first and then nodded. "Everything is fine, just like I said."

Cari wondered who he had really texted. It wasn't like Bob to lie, but she was fairly certain he had not been texting Chris.

"Okay, great. Once we get off the plane, we're renting a car, right?"

"Yes," Bob said a bit distractedly.

"And then lunch?"

"And then lunch."

The plane taxied to the gate and after a few minutes, they were able to stand up to exit the aircraft. Cari grabbed her suitcase from the overhead bin and followed the other passengers off the plane with Bob behind her. Once they were in the airport, she fished around in her bag for her cell phone.

"I'm going to give Grandmother a call while we make our way to the rental car area," she told Bob.

"I read online that we don't have to take a shuttle to another location; the rental cars are onsite."

"Awesome."

She pulled her phone out and unlocked it. After taking it out of airplane mode, she found her grandmother in her contacts list and hit the call button. She answered on the first ring.

"Cari! I kept thinking you would call. How are you, my dear? And *where* are you?"

Cari laughed. "Hi, Grandmother. I'm doing well. I'm in Minneapolis with Bob."

"Minneapolis! Wow! I bet it's beautiful there. Are you going to see the Great Lakes?"

"Well, all I know so far is that we're going to see one of them: Lake Superior," Cari told her. "I did get to see all of them from the plane, though."

"This is quite an adventure that boy has planned for you. Where are you headed next?"

"I'm not sure, but I'm excited to get there."

"Well, I've been busy getting everything ready for my little greats to get here later today. Hilary has been calling me every night to tell me about all the things she wants to do."

"I know they're excited to see you again."

"Not as excited as I am. Now, you be sure to send me photos of your adventures and let me know where you are once you get there."

"I will, Grandmother. I love you."

"I love you more."

* * * * *

Lydia smiled at one of her guests as they passed each other on the narrow staircase. The bed and breakfast only had two rooms on the top floor. Both were considered to be suites with their own balconies. She had reserved the one with the better view of Lake Superior for her nephew Bob and had just finished getting the room in order for their arrival later that afternoon. She was looking forward to his visit and the opportunity to meet his girlfriend.

She passed by the welcoming desk and continued outside to the mailbox to collect her mail. She sighed when she saw the state tax assessor's return address on one of the envelopes. Her property taxes had continued to increase seemingly exponentially over the last few years. She knew people sometimes protested their tax assessments, but she wasn't familiar with the process. If Harvey were still alive, he would know what to do.

Her late husband had run the bed and breakfast alongside her throughout their marriage in addition to working as a CPA at a public accounting firm in Duluth. He had been her handyman and business manager of sorts until his pancreatic cancer diagnosis a few years ago. Harvey had gone through numerous rounds of chemo and radiation as well as surgery, but in the end, it wasn't enough. Thankfully, his "real" job had good health insurance or his treatments would have left them completely broke. Even good health insurance isn't enough with cancer. Eventually, you reach the experimental stage of treatments and nothing is covered. As it was, she still needed to find creative ways to cut costs to keep the bed and breakfast afloat. These tax increases were threatening to take it all away. When Harvey's insurance wouldn't cover some of the experimental treatments, they decided to mortgage the business. It hadn't been an impulsive decision, but she knew they had rushed through the process in order to get the money faster. Now there was a mortgage payment to go along with the property taxes. When she had time, she needed to give the mortgage a second glance.

Lydia knew that her brother Jack could probably help her with all of this tax nonsense, but she hated asking him. He didn't live nearby and had his own problems. Plus, asking him for help meant admitting she couldn't handle the business on her own. She wasn't ready to grovel yet. The bell above the door rang, bringing her back to the present. Lydia glanced up to see a couple entering with their luggage.

"Welcome to The Boarding House. You must be William and Claudia Berk. My name is Lydia. If you'll step over to the desk, I will get you checked in for your stay."

The middle-aged couple rolled their two suitcases up to the desk and smiled at Lydia. The woman's jet-black hair was cut in a bob that framed her pale face. She removed her sunglasses, displaying bright blue eyes with a dusting of freckles across the bridge of her nose. Lydia thought to herself that the woman could easily pass as Snow White if she wore red lipstick. Her husband removed his hat, revealing a smooth head. His skin was as dark as his wife's was pale. He had a warm smile that set Lydia at ease.

"Beautiful building you have here," the man said.

Lydia beamed. "Thank you, Mr. Berk. It's been in my family for several generations."

"We read about its history when we were making our reservations online. We have really been looking forward to this visit," the woman remarked.

"Wonderful! I have you down for three nights with us. I just need to see a photo ID to confirm who you are."

William pulled out his wallet and handed Lydia his driver's license. She quickly matched the name and address to the reservation in her computer and then returned it to him along with a key to their room.

"Here is your room key. You'll be in number six; it's on the second floor. Did you want to make any dinner reservations with our restaurant while you're at the desk?"

"That would be lovely. Do you have anything around six-thirty tonight?" Claudia asked.

Lydia pulled up the reservations app and checked the availability. "I sure do. Let me get you on the list."

She added their names and then swiveled her chair around to face the cabinet behind her. She kept her welcome bags in the bottom cabinet and gave one to every first-time guest.

"Here's a little something I put together for all of my first-time guests. It has a paper map of the area, which includes information about the ferry and other tourist attractions in town. It also has a handful of items from some of our local businesses. If you could just take a moment to sign our guestbook before heading to your room, I would appreciate it. Enjoy your stay!"

"Wow! Thanks so much!" Claudia exclaimed. She grabbed the pen next to the large book and scripted in their names, dates of stay, and hometown.

The couple lifted their suitcases and began climbing the stairs to Lydia's right. She smiled to herself. It always made her happy when her guests were happy. Her smile faded as she remembered the break-in earlier in the week and the taxes looming on the horizon. She sifted through the other mail in her pile and walked over to her office to put the important items in the top drawer of her desk for later. She sighed and checked her watch. Bob should be arriving in the next hour or two based on the texts he had sent her earlier.

Chapter 3

Cari gazed out the window at all the green, rolling hills. She wasn't sure she had ever seen so much open space. She saw horses and cows grazing in some of the fields, but others were vacant. Wildflowers of a variety of colors covered the ditches alongside the road.

"Is it always so green out here?"

Bob nodded. "In the summers it is. In the winter…well, it's pretty frozen up here just like in New York."

"You've been here in the wintertime? I thought you grew up near Chicago."

"I did, but…"

"But what?"

"I guess it's time to let you know where we're going."

Cari leaned forward in anticipation.

"We're headed to Harborville, Wisconsin. My family has owned and operated a bed and breakfast there for several generations. We used to celebrate Christmas there every year when I was a child."

Cari clapped her hands. "Oh wow! That's so exciting. Several generations, huh? How many?"

Bob shrugged sheepishly. "I should know the answer to that question, but I've forgotten. It goes back to the gold rush, if I remember correctly…Grandfather Willoughby was the original owner of the business."

"That's incredible. Grandfather Willoughby! I love it. It's still in your family, so who is running it now? Your parents are still in Chicago, right?"

"They are. My dad's big sister, Lydia owns it now. It usually passes down to the oldest child, though occasionally, it skips over a generation. In fact, Lydia inherited it from my great-grandfather. None of his children were interested in running the place, so he just kept at it until Lydia was out of college and married."

"*And* married?" Cari asked.

"Don't take it the wrong way. Aunt Lydia didn't need to be married to inherit the place. She just happened to get married right after she graduated from college."

Cari nodded. "What a cool thing to have in your family. Imagine all the memories tied up in that place. Who will your aunt and uncle pass the business onto?"

Bob bit his lip. "Well, Uncle Harvey passed away last year—"

"Oh, I'm so sorry. How terrible."

"He had pancreatic cancer. It was pretty bad."

"Do they not have children?" Cari asked hesitantly.

"No, they do. Their daughter is a professional ballerina—"

"Oh wow! That's really neat. Where does she dance?"

"She's with the Toronto Ballet right now."

"So, she's probably not going to take over the business…"

Bob grinned. "Probably not, but her younger brother might. He's studying business in college. He'll be a junior this fall, but he's doing some sort of study abroad program in Europe this summer."

"That seems like good experience. I'm really excited to see the bed and breakfast, Bob! What a great surprise!"

Bob smiled. "I'm really excited to show it to you. I've made reservations for all sorts of activities on the lake too. Kayaking, a lighthouse tour, a ferry trip—"

"Now I know why we needed a whole week for this trip!" she laughed.

Bob steered the rental car around a curve and Cari gasped. Lake Superior was in full view. The sun was shining, making the lake shimmer and sparkle.

"That's amazing. What a view!" she exclaimed.

Bob grinned and blushed a bit. "Wait until you see our view from the bed and breakfast tomorrow. The sunrises here are indescribable."

A road sign indicated that Harborville was just ahead. Cari continued to stare at the lake in awe. They passed a sign indicating that Harborville was home to just over four thousand people. Restaurants and touristy shops dotted the streets. Bob was no longer using the GPS to navigate; Cari could tell he knew where he was going.

"How many years has it been since you were out here?"

He rubbed his chin thoughtfully. "I would say five or six. I think I last visited right after graduating from NYU."

They continued down the hill towards Lake Superior. When they were just a block or two from the shoreline, Bob turned into a small parking lot next to a three-story house. Cari craned her neck to read the sign hanging from a post in the front yard: The Boarding House.

"This is it?" she asked.

"This is it. The Boarding House. Originally, it *was* more of a boarding house than a bed and breakfast. People would rent rooms here for half a week, a week, or possibly longer depending on their circumstances."

They pulled their bags from the trunk of the vehicle and Bob locked it. Cari pulled out her phone to take a picture of the large house. The trim was painted a light beige that complemented the dark red bricks well. She could see a large flower garden in the backyard and hoped they could check it out later.

"Are you ready?" Bob asked, tilting his head toward the front of the building.

She grinned. "It looks lovely. I'm excited to see the inside. Let's get another photo together before we go in, though."

Bob nodded in agreement and stood next to her. The sign for The Boarding House was on the awning behind them. Cari snapped the photo and then put her phone back in her bag. She followed him to the front door. Just as he was about to open it, a petite woman with shoulder-length, curly grey hair bounded out the door. She had on glasses with bright red frames. Her sparkling blue eyes matched Bob's to a tee.

"Bob! You made it!" She turned to Cari. "And you must be Cari. It is wonderful to meet you. I'm so happy to have you as a guest for your vacation."

She grabbed Cari's suitcase and wheeled it inside, talking the entire way. Cari tried to keep up with everything she was saying.

"...I'm so glad your flight in was uneventful. How were the roads? You never know when someone's animal is going to get out or when you're going to get stuck behind a tractor."

"Everything was great, Aunt Lydia. Cari, this is my Aunt Lydia. She is the owner and operator of the bed and breakfast."

Lydia blushed. "Oh, forgive me! I didn't tell you my name. I'm just so excited for you to be here."

She left Cari's suitcase near the stairs and sat down behind the desk. Cari noticed a large, old-fashioned guestbook with rows of signatures on the counter in front of them. Skimming through the names, she noticed four other couples and one single occupant would be calling "The Boarding House" home while she and Bob were visiting. Lydia continued to prattle on and Cari tried to focus again on what the woman was saying.

20

"...top floor. It has the best view of our Lake. You will love it. Here are your keys. Bob, you said that you wanted to eat here several nights during your stay. I penciled you in for around seven each evening. Let me know which days you want to keep and we'll get it all settled."

"Thank you, Aunt Lydia. I'll come back down in a few minutes with the meal plan, okay?"

"Don't forget to sign my book, dear." She smiled at them from behind the desk.

Cari picked up the fountain pen and wrote their names on the first empty line, listing Brenington as their hometown. She continued to take in her surroundings as she began following Bob up the stairs: the hardwood floors, the old-fashioned wallpaper, the hand carved banister. The house had been well taken care of. She wondered how often it needed renovations or repairs.

Cari found herself a bit short of breath when they reached the third floor. The stairs were rather steep. Bob inserted the key into the doorknob of the room on the right and swung the door open. There was a full bathroom just to the left with a large, garden bathtub beneath a window across from the door. A king-sized bed was positioned to her right. Across from the bed were two loveseat sofas and a coffee table. She could see the balcony from another large window further to her right. She abandoned her suitcase near the bed and crossed the room to the balcony door. The window blinds were closed, but she could see the afternoon sun peeking through the edges. She unlocked the door and stepped onto the balcony. It wrapped around the corner of the building. The lake sparkled in the sunlight. She saw several sailboats on the lake as well as some people in kayaks. It looked very peaceful.

"It's amazing, Bob. What a beautiful place!" She called back to him. "Come look!"

Bob stepped outside after double-checking that the door wouldn't lock them out. As he took her hand, he said, "It's pretty great, huh? I'm glad you like it."

"I can't believe we get to stay here for a week. Genevieve is going to be so jealous!"

"Speaking of Genevieve, didn't she start her training program this week too?"

"That's right! She did. I should send her a text and see how her week is going."

"O'Zook's might go out of business without the two of you in town."

Cari laughed. "We do go there a lot. Oh, I need to call Grandmother. I promised I would tell her where we ended up."

* * * * *

"Cari! I'm so excited to find out where you are!" her grandmother exclaimed.

"I'm in Wisconsin, in a little town called Harborville. It's right on Lake Superior."

"How wonderful! Send me lots of photos…oh, your sister says to send her photos too," she said delightedly. "Where are you staying?"

"It turns out that Bob's family has a bed and breakfast out here. It was once a boarding house, but that was during the gold rush. He said that it's been in his family for several generations."

"Wow! What an heirloom. Send us a picture of that too."

"I will. How is Bea?"

Her grandmother paused before answering. "She seems happy, but she's hiding something. Don't worry; I'll get it out of her before she leaves."

Cari smiled. "Give everyone my love. I better get back to unpacking."

"We love you too, sweet girl."

The call ended and Cari opened her phone's camera to take a picture of their view. Bob had gone back inside while she was speaking with Grandmother. She did her best to get a panoramic image and then sent it off to her friend. Genevieve hadn't shared her schedule for the training program, so Cari hoped she hadn't interrupted anything or gotten her friend in trouble. Before she could worry further, her phone buzzed with an incoming call. *Genevieve!*

"Gen! I didn't expect you to call. How are you?"

"I'm doing really well. This program is amazing. We've barely started, but they gave us an overview of the whole thing on Monday and I'm really learning a lot already."

"Are there active FBI agents leading it?" Cari asked.

"Active? Well, I don't know that they are currently active in the field. Most of them seem older, like maybe they have transitioned to a desk job. They were all active agents at some point though."

"That's great. Did they say anything about the recruitment process following the program?"

"Well, they sort of hand-waved that part. They said that in special cases, they have recruited people to the FBI from this program, but it's pretty rare." Genevieve admitted with a hint of disappointment.

"I'm sure once they see you in action, they'll see you're definitely worth their time," Cari said encouragingly.

"Thanks. If nothing else, they at least know my name now. But that's not why I called. Where are you? That view is incredible!"

"It's Lake Superior! Bob and I are staying at a B&B out here. Isn't it gorgeous?"

"The lake is beautiful. I'll have to add that to my must-see list. Did you say a B&B? Sounds like things are getting serious with Bob, huh?" Genevieve teased.

Cari felt herself blushing and grinned. "I don't deserve him, but I'm happy to be with him."

"Keep sending me photos. I will enjoy your vacation vicariously."

"I will. Don't be a stranger. I can't believe I'll hardly see you for a month."

"I'll do my best…I'll still be around on the weekends, though. Gotta run. Bye, Cari." She ended the call.

Cari left the balcony and set her phone on the dresser. Bob was nowhere to be seen; she figured he must have gone downstairs to speak with his aunt. She put her suitcase up on the bed and unzipped it. They planned to stay here for the whole trip, so she decided to get her clothing into the dresser rather than live out of the suitcase. The room had a closet, so she hung up her dress before it wrinkled any worse than it already had. It didn't take long to get her clothing put away. She finished unpacking just as the door to their room opened.

"Hey, Cari. How was your grandmother?"

"She was really excited to hear about our trip. I talked to Genevieve too. Where have you been?"

"I went back down to talk to Aunt Lydia. On our way in, I noticed the windows in the dining hall were being replaced and wanted to ask her about it. I also got all of our dinner reservations squared away for the restaurant here."

"How often does she have to do renovations? It's such a lovely building, but I'm sure it requires regular maintenance."

"I don't really know. She said that she was in the process of gradually replacing the windows on all the floors. They should be more energy efficient."

"That's good. I'm sure it gets pretty cold here in the winter."

"Are you ready to do some exploring? We don't have dinner reservations for over an hour."

"Sure! I noticed the flower garden in the back when we pulled into the parking lot. Can we look at that first?" She grabbed her phone off the dresser and slipped it into her pocket.

"Let's do it."

Bob locked the door behind them and started to put the key in his pocket.

"Before I forget, we have two keys to the room. Aunt Lydia gave me the other one when I was downstairs earlier." He handed Cari the key.

"It has been such a long time since I've stayed somewhere with metal keys! I've really gotten used to the key cards, you know?"

"They are definitely something from the past."

Cari led the way down the narrow staircase and past the front desk. Lydia was no longer seated behind the desk. She glanced toward the dining room and saw Lydia watching the men replacing the windows. The woman had to wear a lot of different hats to keep this business running.

Once outside, Bob took Cari's hand and directed her to the back of the house where a gated fence encircled the garden. A stone path cut through the center, separating the flowers from the vegetables.

"I wish I knew more about gardening. These flowers are so lovely. I could never keep them alive, but they're just beautiful." Cari pulled out her phone to take photos of the colorful flowers.

"These are zinnias, and you probably recognize sunflowers, right?" Bob asked as he pointed at the flowers.

Cari laughed. "Yes, I can name a sunflower."

"They use a lot of the vegetables from the garden at the restaurant."

"That's so cool. Genevieve would be fascinated. Did you know that she grows vegetables and stuff in her apartment's garden? It's a rooftop garden."

Bob raised his eyebrows. "I wonder who is maintaining it for her while she's doing the training program."

"She is. The program is in the city, so she just has a bit of a drive every day."

Bob nodded. They followed the little path around the corner. A myriad of rosebushes greeted them. Cari's eyes were drawn to a gap near the bay window. She couldn't get too close because the rosebushes were well-established and she didn't want to get scratched by a thorn.

"That second to last bush doesn't have any blooms on it. I wonder why." Cari pointed.

Bob took a step closer and leaned in. He was taller than Cari and could see over the bushes better. "It looks like it has a branch broken off. There are flowers lower, but I think there might be more to the window story."

Bob's face darkened a bit and Cari wondered what was troubling him. She looked through the window and saw Lydia walking away. Before she could ask, Bob shook his head and smiled at Cari.

"Is everything okay?" she asked.

"I'm not sure, but let's not worry about it right now. I'll check with Aunt Lydia later. The garden only has one way in and out, so we'll have to retrace our steps to get back to the street."

Cari followed Bob back through the garden to the parking lot. Several other people were walking along the sidewalk and she wondered if they were tourists too, or locals out for a stroll. As they made their way down the road toward Lake Superior, Cari noticed herself leaning back to keep herself upright. She hadn't realized it before, but all of the streets sloped down in the direction of the lake. When she thought back to their drive into town, she remembered the roads being windy, but hadn't paid attention to their steep descent.

The cobblestone streets were lined with little shops and restaurants. They all had a lake or seaside theme to their names. Bob walked with his hands in his pockets, seemingly oblivious to his surroundings.

"Something on your mind?"

"Hmm?" Bob asked absentmindedly. "Oh, sorry. I was just thinking about...something."

Cari smiled. "I can tell. Is everything okay?"

"It's fine. I'm sorry. Look, we're almost to the pier," he pointed ahead.

"The lake is enormous. I mean, I know they're called the Great Lakes and everything, but I never realized *how big* they are. The sunlight makes the water shimmer. It's amazing. I almost can't believe I'm here." Cari reached over and hugged Bob.

Bob smiled. "I'm glad you like it. I know it isn't really a beach vacation, but I think it will still be a fun place to relax."

"Did you ever fish out here as a child?"

Bob choked back a laugh. "I mean, people in my family would fish, but it wasn't really a strength of mine. I once got the fish hook stuck in my ear and my grandpa had to...well, let's just say this scar on my ear is not one to be proud of."

"Ouch! Just thinking about that makes my ear hurt," Cari said, pulling on her own ear.

Cari looked out across the lake at the sailboats. The sun was peeking between their sails as it grew closer to sunset. A light breeze blew her hair into her face, so she pulled it back using an elastic she had on her wrist. The seagulls resting on the pilings watched as they made their way down the pier. She wondered how often people fed them since they seemed completely unbothered by their presence. They reminded her of the birds in "Finding Nemo" who chanted "Mine, mine, mine" over and over again.

Cari heard a phone vibrate and glanced at Bob. He had his phone out and was frowning as he thumbed off a text to someone.

He wasn't usually so secretive. She turned back to the lake and decided to take some photos while Bob was preoccupied. She knew Grandmother would love to see the sun setting beyond the lake and did her best with her phone camera.

"We should probably head back to the house." Bob startled her.

"What time is our reservation?"

"Seven-thirty—I asked Aunt Lydia to shift it down a bit so that we could do a little exploring."

"Let's get a photo together first, then we can get back to the Boarding House."

Bob acquiesced and joined her. She grabbed a photo of them with a sailboat in the distance.

"Thanks for being a good sport with all the photos."

He smiled and gave her a quick kiss. "I'm glad you're enjoying Wisconsin. Ready to go back up? It's virtually uphill the whole way, so it will take us a little longer."

"It is *really* steep. I noticed the pitch of the streets when we were walking down here. It could be a bit challenging to go running tomorrow."

Bob chuckled initially and then furrowed his brow. "Oh, are we still on the running plan here?"

"The flame out 5k is just a few weeks away! You don't want to lose your progress now," she teased.

"I should have planned this trip for after the race. Running here might kill me."

Cari laughed as she hooked her arm in his to walk back up to the bed and breakfast. She was excited to try the restaurant at The Boarding House. The dining room had an equally beautiful view of the lake, so they would be able to watch the full sunset while they ate.

Chapter 4

C ari took a sip of her cocktail and returned it to its coaster. The sun was just about to drop below the horizon. She wanted to grab a photo of it before it was gone.

"I'm going to step outside and snap a quick photo of the sunset. I'll be right back," she told Bob.

He nodded in her direction, but she could see his mind was a million miles away. She hurried outside and pulled her phone from her pocket. Because the lake was so much lower than the bed and breakfast, she could easily capture the image without needing to crop out cars or stand on her toes to see around other buildings. She took a few photos and then looked back at the window. The sun was glaring off the glass, so she could only sort of see inside. Their table was right by the bay window, so she should have been able to see Bob's upper body. Instead, the table looked deserted. She frowned and wondered why Bob had left.

She quickly sent the photos to Bea, Genevieve, and Grandmother as she walked along the sidewalk. When she stepped inside the house, she saw Bob getting up from the floor behind their table. She quickly walked over and tilted her head at him.

"What in the world are you doing, Bob?"

He flinched and then blushed. "I didn't see you walk back inside. Did you get some nice photos?"

"Did you lose something under the table?"

"What? Oh, I uh, dropped my…knife."

She frowned, but didn't question him. "I got some really good photos."

"Here comes the waiter with our appetizer. We can look at the photos later."

The waiter set down a small plate of crab cakes on top of a bed of arugula. Cari scooped one off the plate onto her own and took a bite.

"These are amazing."

"Would you like a second cocktail or are you ready for the wine you ordered?"

Bob looked at Cari, who shrugged her indifference. "Let's go ahead and switch to the wine now."

"I'll be right back with your glasses, then."

Cari took another bite of the crab cake. "I can't wait to taste the seafood pasta dish I ordered. Does your aunt do all of the cooking too?"

"Oh no. I think that ended with my great-grandmother. They have a full-time chef. He also oversees the garden. They get some of their vegetables from a local farmers market this time of year too. During the winter, they have to have things shipped in, of course."

"So, what is the plan tomorrow, after we go running, that is."

"Right," Bob said slowly. "After the running…I thought we could eat breakfast here—we don't need a reservation as it's only available to Boarding House guests. Then, I made us a kayaking reservation. It's self-guided, but we will get some basic instructions on how to maneuver the kayak before taking off on our own."

"Fun! Have you done a lot of kayaking?"

"It's been a few years, but I can stay afloat."

"I did some canoeing at summer camp as a kid. Hopefully, that will count for something."

"I'm hoping to take you around to some of the caves along the shoreline. The water from the lake has carved out a bunch of caves over the years."

"Are there animals in the caves? Like bats?"

"I don't think so. I guess there could be fish, of course. When the tide comes in—"

"Lakes have tides?"

"Yes. Anyway, when the tide comes in, the caves fill with water, so it would be a challenge for a non-aquatic being to use one as their home."

"Fascinating. It sounds like fun."

They finished the crab cakes and set the plate aside for their waiter to grab. Cari licked her lips in satisfaction. Before she could ask Bob what other surprises he had up his sleeve, Lydia arrived at their table with their entrees. Bob started to get up from the table.

"No you don't!" Lydia said sternly. "I just wanted to bring your food over myself and see how everything is tasting."

Bob settled back into his seat as Cari responded. "Everything is amazing, Lydia. The cocktails, the food, the view—it's incredible."

Lydia beamed at her. "Thank you, my dear. I'm thrilled to have you here."

"It's all really great, Aunt Lydia."

"Here are your entrees. The asparagus came straight from our garden and we got the heirloom tomatoes from Contessa's. Do you remember Contessa, Bob?"

Cari thought she noticed Bob's cheeks redden in response to his aunt's question. He cleared his throat. "I do."

"Well, can I get you anything before I return to the office? Second glass of wine, perhaps?"

"Nothing for me. Thank you again, Lydia," Cari responded warmly.

Bob shook his head and Lydia retreated from their table. Rather than question Bob about Contessa, Cari decided to dig into her fettuccine with salmon and a side of asparagus. Bob had ordered a local fish, the whitefish. She had never had it before and decided she would have to try it before their vacation ended.

"Any other surprises for me on this trip?"

Bob coughed as he choked on his bite. He gulped down some water and swallowed a few times before speaking. "Surprises? Uh, listen. Contessa was, is…just someone that used to spend time with our family sometimes when we would visit. She owns another bed and breakfast type place in one of the neighboring towns."

Cari bit the inside of her cheek to keep from laughing at Bob's awkwardness. "I meant besides kayaking."

Relief washed over Bob's face. "Oh, of course. Yes, um, surprises. Um. I thought you might enjoy taking the ferry over to Specter Island one day."

"That sounds ominous."

He smiled. "It's a lot of folklore, but there are some fun hikes and a beach we can explore."

"Do people swim in the lake?"

"It's pretty cold, but some people will do it. If it's sunny out, you can warm up pretty quickly after you dry off."

"I'll hold off on the swimming decision for now."

They finished their entrees and Bob signed the check over to their room. Cari had thought about getting dessert, but she was too full to eat anymore. She made a mental note to skip the appetizer next time so she had room to try the key lime pie. Maybe their kayaking adventure would work up a bigger appetite.

* * * * *

32

Cari bent down to tie the laces on her running shoes. Bob had slept fitfully the night before and almost seemed relieved that it was morning. It was just barely morning. Cari had requested they get up early so they could see the sunrise. Harborville's position on Lake Superior allowed them to see the sunrise over the lake too. Bob rubbed his eyes and then pulled a bottle of water out of his backpack and took a sip.

"Ready to take on these hills, Mr. Hursley?" she asked him.

"As ready as I'll ever be. I can't believe I let you and Genevieve talk me into this."

"Don't forget Chris."

"I have the worst co-workers ever. Runimoss is smarter than all of us." Bob said, referencing Genevieve's partner, Alex Runimoss.

"Is he the race starter?"

"No, that's the fire chief. Halpin. Runimoss is handing out water at the finish line, which is shaded."

"It's only three miles. You'll be fine."

"Three point one."

"Here we go."

After locking their room, they made their way outside. Cari thought the road might have gotten steeper overnight. It wasn't going to be the easiest morning run she'd ever done. She looked at Bob, who nodded his consent, and they took off up the hill.

"Think of how easy it will be on our way back."

He grunted. "You know what's easier? Not running at all."

"A mile and a half up and then a mile and a half down. You'll be fine."

Her watch kept track of their pace and distance. She was breathing hard already and knew that Bob must be struggling too. Her subconscious told her that the roads would level out after a few turns, but as they wound their way out of town, the road just kept going up. Bob grunted again and stopped.

"This is insane. I'm just walking today."

"C'mon. You can do this. We've barely gone a third of a mile!" she encouraged him.

"Nope. I can hardly catch my breath. Just walking up these hills is hard. I'll catch up to you on the downhill."

She looked at her watch and saw that her pace was significantly slower than usual, but she was determined to run the whole way. Chris had started this whole thing by claiming that he could outrun Genevieve. Bob probably regretted joining the conversation, but he had jumped in to say that Cari could probably beat them both. This led to Chris proposing they all sign up for the Fourth of July 5k and the losers would buy the winner dinner that night. Cari suspected it was Chris' way of trying to get Genevieve to go on a date with him. He didn't realize that she was very quietly dating a firefighter. She looked at her watch again. She had almost made it a mile. The road just kept going up. She felt like she was barely going faster than walking and hoped it would level out soon.

She resisted the urge to bend over and catch her breath when she finally reached the halfway point. Turning back and running downhill was a bit terrifying. The road was so steep. She had to pay close attention to her footing as she quickly moved back down the road. She caught up to Bob with a little less than a mile to go. He turned around, but kept walking.

"I thought you were going to run downhill?"

"I was, but I think I might fall, so I'm going to keep walking. I'll catch up to you at the house."

* * * * *

Cari stumbled to a halt in front of the bed and breakfast. She pulled their room key from her pocket as she walked up the porch steps. At least it was cool out. She only ran three or four days a week, and it seemed like she would go with three a week while they were in Harborville. Her legs protested climbing the stairs to their room, but she finally made it. She started to stick the key into the lock but then realized the door was slightly ajar. She knew Bob couldn't have beaten her back and wondered if the maid was already cleaning.

"Hello? Is anyone there?" she called out as she started to step inside.

The door pushed back against her, almost knocking her down. Startled, she pushed back, and the door swung freely open. She heard the balcony door open and looked just in time to see a man swing himself over the side. Gasping, Cari raced over to the balcony door wondering what he had stolen.

She leaned over the railing, but didn't see anyone. The house had a rose trellis to the right, though only ivy was growing on it at the moment. She could see a few broken vines and assumed the man must have climbed down in his retreat from their room.

"Cari?" Bob shouted from inside the room.

"I'm out here, Bob!"

"You left the door—what's wrong?"

Cari swallowed. "Someone broke into our room while we were out running. I startled the intruder on my way inside."

Bob's face went white. "Are you okay? I'm so sorry."

"I'm fine. I didn't get a very good look at him. This sounds cliché, but it happened so fast. I thought maybe the maid service was cleaning our room. I didn't want to startle anyone, so I announced myself as I opened the door. That was rewarded with the door getting pushed back into my face and I barely saw him climbing over the balcony railing after I got inside. He might have passed you on the sidewalk on your way to the house. Did you see anyone?"

Bob started frantically going through his things. "I saw a few people. I don't know. We need to go talk to Aunt Lydia."

"Did he steal something? You look a little freaked out," Cari asked him.

Bob visibly relaxed after going through the pockets of his suitcase. She wondered if he was looking for his wallet.

"No, thankfully everything is here, but we need to let Aunt Lydia know," Bob told her.

"Can I take a shower first?"

"I'll give her a call and ask if we can chat with her downstairs, okay?"

"I'll be fast."

"I'll gather up our things for kayaking after I call Aunt Lydia. That way, we won't need to come back up here before we leave," Bob told her.

"Sounds good." She grabbed a change of clothes from the dresser and hurried into the bathroom.

* * * * *

Lydia's eyes filled with tears as she recounted the break-ins to The Boarding House that had occurred over the last month. She had almost dropped her cell phone when Bob called asking to talk and reported the intruder. She wrung her hands in her lap as the young couple seated across from her listened to her tales.

"Again, I am so sorry. The other break-ins have all been in the middle of the night. They've broken a window or two, but it doesn't seem like they are stealing anything."

"Have you reported it to the police?"

Lydia cringed. "Yes, but as I said, nothing was stolen, so they aren't really doing anything. I haven't kept it from the guests either...I mean, except for you two. I'm sorry."

"Can you request that the police patrol the neighborhood more frequently?"

Lydia bit her lip, almost afraid to respond. "I guess I could, but I feel like that just reminds people that I've had break-ins and would make them less likely to stay. I'm already losing business over this." She paused. "I said nothing has been stolen. They didn't steal from you, did they?"

Bob shook his head. "Everything is where we left it. We were only gone for half an hour or so."

"That's right. I didn't see anyone outside when we first left the house either," Cari agreed.

Lydia started to say something when someone knocked on the door. "I think that's the kitchen staff with your breakfast. I know you're going kayaking today and didn't want you to get a late start because of this. I called over to the kitchen to have some scones brought over." She paused. "Becky? Come on in."

A young woman with an apron entered the office. Lydia marveled at how she balanced the tray of scones and water and opened the door at the same time. Becky set the tray on Lydia's desk.

"I brought you ice water too, but would you like anything else? Juice, coffee, mimosa?"

"Coffee would be lovely. Thank you so much," Cari responded.

"Cream and sugar?" Becky asked.

"Any chance you have honey and milk?" Cari grinned.

"I can do that. I'll be right back. And you, sir?"

"Black coffee is fine for me," Bob told her.

Becky backed out of the office. Lydia looked at Bob, trying to remember where they were in the conversation.

"I'm sorry. Where were we?"

"The break-ins. What did the police do?"

"They didn't find anything. Like I said, it's been hard on the business too. I've had people cancel their reservations."

"I guess that is to be expected. Do you have a security system? Cameras? Some sort of alarm?"

Lydia dropped her head and sighed. "I know I've been irresponsible with how I've handled this. I just thought it was a one-off and whoever it was would realize that there was nothing of value here. I can't afford to lose any more business, but an alarm and camera system sounds expensive."

"I understand that Aunt Lydia, but put yourself in your guest's shoes. Knowing there is a system keeping the building secure— that's tied directly to the police department—it's a comfort. It might deter your burglar too."

"I should have gotten an alarm system ages ago. It's just an added expense..." she trailed off. Before she could add to her statement, a knock at the door announced Becky's return with the coffee.

"Do you know any of the officers with the local police department? Someone who would listen to you?" Bob asked her as Cari stirred the honey and milk into her coffee.

"Harborville doesn't have its own department. There's state police and the county sheriff's office...oh, and the neighboring town has a local police department."

"Who has come out when you've reported the break-ins in the past?"

"You're going to think I'm an idiot. I don't know. I just kept hoping it would stop. I didn't write any of it down. I'm such a fool."

Cari patted Lydia's hand from across the desk. "Let me call Detective Runimoss. He's my best friend's partner back in New York. I'm supposed to be keeping tabs on him while she's off doing some training anyway." She grabbed her coffee and a scone and stood up.

"He's not going to come all the way out here!" Lydia protested.

Bob interjected as Cari excused herself to make the phone call. "No, Aunt Lydia. He's not going to come here. He's been in law enforcement a long time. He might know someone out here who could help us." He blew on his coffee and took a sip.

Lydia grabbed Bob's hand. "I'm so sorry, Bob. I can't believe my stubbornness almost resulted in harm to Cari. I would never forgive—"

"Aunt Lydia! You can't keep beating yourself up like this. She is just fine. And Cari is resourceful. She has helped the police solve numerous crimes—even murder, back in Brenington. It's okay."

Lydia released Bob's hand. He cleared his throat and she could tell his mind was working through all the details of what needed to happen. He drummed his fingers on her desk for a moment before looking at her again.

"Aunt Lydia, how bad is it?"

"How bad is what?"

"The business. You've mentioned money trouble and people canceling reservations," he said gently.

"Money is pretty tight. When Harvey got sick, we had to really pinch pennies. We mortgaged the business to pay for his treatments. I'm not behind on payments, but if people keep canceling their reservations...."

Bob tried to hide his shock, but Lydia could see it in his eyes. "I can see you feel overwhelmed. Have you talked to dad?"

"I've picked up the phone to call Jack and tell him all this, but I can't bring myself to do it. He'll be so disappointed in me."

"Aunt Lydia, no. He can help. We're all in this together, okay?"

* * * * *

Cari stepped outside and went to the garden to call Alex. She hoped he would answer. Genevieve told her that Cari's former co-worker, Lionel Cardian had really jaded Alex against the media and all journalists. Over the last eighteen months, she had worked to win his favor. She hit send on his number as she sat down on the garden bench. She nibbled on the scone while willing him to pick up. *Answer, answer, answer...*

"Well, hello, Ms. Turnlyle. To what do I owe the pleasure?" Alex asked sardonically.

"Alex! I'm so glad you answered. Listen. Bob and I are out in Wisconsin—"

"Blah, blah, blah. Can you get to the point?" Alex interrupted.

Cari tried not to be impatient. *She could get to the point faster if he didn't interrupt!* "Here's the deal. Bob's aunt owns this bed and breakfast out here in Wisconsin and we just learned she has had several break-ins over the last month. Is there any chance that you know someone out here we can work with to have this investigated?"

"Wisconsin? I mean, can't you just call the local station? Surely you know how to use Google."

Cari took a breath before responding. Alex could be so irritating. "She is trying to keep this from running up the rumor mill and ruining her business. Do you know anyone who can be somewhat discreet?"

Alex let out a sigh. Cari could picture him rolling his eyes. "Where in Wisconsin?"

"Harborville. Do you need me to spell it?"

"Do I look like an idiot to you? Just a second. Let me look up the person's info. I might know someone nearby."

Cari rubbed her locket subconsciously while she waited for Alex to respond. She wondered what her grandmother would say when she told her about the break-in. The area seemed so serene. It was hard to couple that with a criminal.

"Well, isn't it a small world. I do know someone out there. Janice Maruthers. She's the local sheriff. I met her at the academy a hundred years ago. She was one of my instructors."

40

Cari frowned. The woman must be close to eighty if she was Alex's instructor. "Uh, are you sure she isn't retired?"

"How old do you think I am?" Alex retorted.

"Uh, not that old. Never mind. Can you text me her contact information and maybe put in a good word for us?"

"What is the aunt's name?"

"Lydia. I guess I don't know her last name." Cari cringed at the realization.

"That's fine. Everyone knows everyone out there, I'm sure."

"Thank so much, Alex. How are things going without Genevieve around?"

"Well, they're pairing me up with some idiot rookie detective who doesn't know...anything. He keeps trying to teach me how to use a computer like I don't know what one is. Fool."

Cari stifled a giggle. "Well, good luck with that. It must feel good to know they trust you to train a rookie, right?"

"Whatever. It's not my first time. Let me know if you need anything else."

"Will do. Thanks again, Alex."

She ended the call and got up from the bench. Before slipping her phone back into her pocket, she scrolled through her contacts. Her thumb hovered over her grandmother's name. She bit the inside of her lip with indecision. She didn't like keeping things from her grandmother, but she needed to tell Bob and Lydia what she'd learned. Just as she closed the phone's call app, a text came in from Alex with Sheriff Maruther's contact info. She thumbed off a thank you text and put the phone back in her pocket.

* * * * *

The door to Lydia's office was closed when Cari got back inside. She started to just walk in without knocking and then second-guessed herself. What if she was interrupting something?

She lifted her hand to knock, though she was tempted to eavesdrop first.

"It's me!" she called out as she knocked on the door.

"Come on in, Cari," Lydia responded.

Before she could twist the knob, the door popped open. Bob had reached over to open it from his chair. They both looked at her expectantly as she retook her seat.

"I talked to Alex, uh, Detective Runimoss. He knows the sheriff out here, um, Janice Maruthers. He sent me her info, but he's also going to call her and let her know we're looking for help."

Cari watched as Lydia's shoulders relaxed. "Thank you so much, Cari. I don't think I've met Ms., uh, Sheriff Maruthers, but I'm glad your friend knows someone out here. Do you think she could recommend a security company to me?"

"Aunt Lydia, we can probably do a Google search for that," Bob interjected.

"The sheriff might know someone local who is trustworthy and cost-efficient." Cari agreed with Lydia. "Here's her contact information. Do you want us to stick around while you call her?"

"Oh no. I don't want to spoil your vacation any more than I already have. I'm a big girl. I can do this."

Bob looked at Cari before responding. She nodded, knowing what he was about to say. "It's no trouble. We would be happy to help you speak with the sheriff."

"No, no, no. This is your vacation. Go, have fun. I'll take care of this. If I have a question, I have your number."

"Do you need a room key back?" Cari asked her.

Lydia blushed and dipped her head before responding. "It's not that I don't trust the two of you, but I have an extra key to every room, plus a master key that will work. You would be surprised how often people lock themselves out. I think I'll call Contessa too and see if she has had any issues with break-ins."

Bob frowned but Cari said, "Okay, then. Let us know if you need anything. We won't be too far away to help."

Chapter 5

J ust as Bob and Cari had stood up to leave, Lydia's landline rang with a call. She mouthed to them it was Sheriff Maruthers and shooed them out the door. Bob paused in the foyer to check for his wallet, phone, and keys.

"Are we all set?" he asked her.

"I have my phone and my room key," she told him.

He exhaled. "It feels weird leaving Aunt Lydia like this, but I guess if she needs us, she'll call."

"Alex assured me that the sheriff is a good cop. She helped train him."

"How is she not retired then?"

"I asked the same thing and it made him mad," Cari laughed.

They walked over to the parking area and Bob paused before unlocking the rental car. He walked the perimeter of the car and then tried the door handles. Finally, he hit the unlock button on the key fob.

"What are you doing?"

"I thought there might be a chance the burglar tried to get into the car too. It seems like he didn't bother with it."

"How can you be sure?" Cari asked cautiously.

"See the rain drops on the door handles? If someone had tried to open the doors, they would have disturbed the water drops."

Cari was impressed. "Well, that's a relief."

"It's also strange that someone would break into a building and leave the cars untouched."

"True. Hopefully, the sheriff can figure out who it is and put a stop to it."

Bob nodded as he placed his backpack in the backseat. "I packed some sunscreen, water, and a few granola bars in the backpack. I also grabbed your floppy hat in case you want to keep the sun off of your face with it."

"Thanks. Good call on the sunscreen *and* the water."

She opened the opposite door and reached for the backpack. Bob grabbed it away first. She pulled her hand back in surprise.

"Did you need something?" he asked quickly, looking sheepish.

"I was just going to get the sunscreen and put it on during the car ride over to the kayak spot. Is that not okay?"

"Oh, no, that's perfectly fine. Here, let me get it for you." He rummaged in the backpack and then handed her the small tube of sunscreen.

"Travel size, huh?"

"It's not like we need a lot."

They got in the car and Bob pulled up directions to the kayaking spot. He tipped the phone her way and she saw it was only a seven-minute drive.

"The route goes along the lake shore, so it's kind of windy. As the crow flies, it's only a couple miles from here," he told her.

He pulled out of the parking lot and followed the directions toward the lake. It was a cloudless day and the lake looked even prettier than the day before. Cari pulled out her phone and took another photo. She watched the seagulls swooping around the shoreline and out across the water as they drove along the road. She slipped her phone back in her pocket and started putting sunscreen on her face, arms, and neck.

"Here we are. Their website said to park off to the side. I think that's over here. I guess they'll tell us if I'm wrong," Bob said slowly. "Let me put on some sunscreen and then we can walk over there."

Cari could see some people near a stack of kayaks and pointed them out to Bob. He finished spreading out his sunscreen and put it back into the backpack. They made their way down the dirt path. Bob pulled out a small plastic bag from his backpack.

"I brought some little bags for our phones so they wouldn't get wet." He handed her the resealable bag and then pulled out another one for himself.

"Good idea." She slipped her phone into the bag and sealed it closed.

"Hi, there. Are you here for the kayak rental?" A woman in a hat and sunglasses asked them. Her wavy grey hair was tied at the back of her neck. Her skin was tanned and leathery making Cari wonder if she spent all day outside during the warmer months. Just past her, a man in a matching hat was helping a family of four into two double kayaks. He zipped some kind of black cover over their legs after they were seated. Cari turned to give her attention to the woman.

"The self-guided tour?" Bob asked.

"That's the one. You must be Bob Hursley." She stuck out her hand to shake theirs. "My name's Dale. Dale McClure. I run the tours here. Have you kayaked before?"

"I have, but it's been a few years."

"I've only been canoeing." Cari shrugged.

"Better than nothing. Let's find you some life jackets and paddles. Then we'll get you squared away in the kayak."

They followed her over to her truck. She opened the passenger door and started rummaging around behind the seats. Eventually, she turned around with two life jackets in her hands.

46

"These should fit. You want them nice and snug," she instructed. "They also have little zipper pockets for your phones, if you want to use them. They aren't totally waterproof, so use it at your own risk."

"Thank you," Cari said as she grabbed hers and shrugged into it. She pulled her phone from her shorts pocket and wedged it into the zippered pocket. It was a tight fit, but it would work. She was glad that Bob thought to bring the plastic bags.

"The paddles are in the truck bed. Just a moment." She unlatched the gate on the truck and reached to grab two paddles. She handed Cari a red one and Bob a yellow one.

"Let's review the strokes first. It's pretty straightforward, but I want to make sure you know all of it before you get out on the water. By the way, I meant to introduce you to my assistant. He was helping the other family into their kayaks when you walked up. He should be finished by the time we get back over there."

Dale grabbed another yellow paddle for herself and demonstrated how to make the kayak turn, how to slow it down, and how to keep it from capsizing. They followed her movements a few times until she seemed to think they were competent enough to take off in one of her boats.

"Okay, if you'll just follow me back over to the lake side, we'll get you in a kayak. You reserved a double, right?"

"That's correct," Bob replied.

They reached the stack of kayaks and Dale and her assistant pulled one down. They positioned it near the water line. Dale waved them over.

"Your backpack might get wet. Is there anything that could get damaged if that happens? If so, you should put it back in your vehicle."

"Actually, it's a waterproof backpack! I got especially for this trip. I only have a few snacks, some bottled water, and sunscreen in case we need to reapply it, plus our hats."

47

"Well, put the hats on!" Dale laughed.

Bob offered Cari her hat and then pulled another one onto his own head. Cari was glad she packed one that tied under her chin. It wasn't super windy, but she was pretty sure her hat would blow away without the ties. She adjusted the strap and then picked her paddle back up. Dale and her assistant made their way back over to Bob and Cari. Dale was carrying two black pieces of fabric.

"This is my assistant, Rich. He'll help you get zipped into the kayak." She handed each of them one of the black items. "These are your skirts. They'll keep your lower body somewhat drier. Not totally dry, but somewhat."

Cari grabbed the thick, black skirt. It had an adjustable waist that she could cinch tighter. She put her paddle back down again and then stepped into the skirt. Bob struggled into his.

Cari giggled. "First time putting on a skirt, Bob?"

His cheeks reddened. "It's been a few years since I've worn one of these—kayaking, of course! I've almost got it."

"Okay, just a few more instructions and then you can get on your way," Dale told them.

They followed Dale and Rich over to the kayak. Rich pushed the nose of the kayak a little further into the lake, then offered his hand to Cari. She carefully stepped into the boat and lowered herself to the seat.

"Bob, when you get into your seat, you'll notice little foot pedals in the foot well. They're called foot braces. You can control the rudder with them. I recommend only doing that if you're really struggling to make her turn."

Bob stepped into the kayak and Cari felt it rock a bit. Rich leaned over her and started zipping her skirt to the boat. She hoped it kept her shorts and feet mostly dry. Looking over her shoulder, she saw Dale reaching to zip Bob's skirt to the kayak too.

"You'll be more comfortable with the backpack in the bulkhead. It will be safe there, I promise."

Cari watched Bob hesitate. Dale must have noticed too. She smirked.

"You're acting like you've got the crown jewels stashed inside there, man. Give it up."

Bob turned crimson and then pulled off the backpack. He handed it to Rich, who stowed it in the bulkhead. "You're right. It's ridiculous to try to wear it over this life jacket. And not very safe."

"Okay, then I think you're all set. My cell phone number is written on both of your paddles. If you get lost or into trouble, just give me a call. Rich is going to follow you out, but he won't be a nuisance. He usually traverses this part of the lake a few times while we have customers out on the water. Honestly, he'll probably stick closer to the family that just pushed off. Do you see that lighthouse off in the distance?" Dale asked them.

Cari squinted across the lake. She thought she might be able to see something that resembled a lighthouse off to the lefthand shore line.

"Over to the left?"

"Yes, ma'am. Don't travel past that. You'll never get back here before dark. Right now, you'll be paddling against the wind on your way out, so if that holds, it won't take you as long to return. No guarantees with the wind, though. Before you reach the lighthouse, you'll run into Specter Island—"

"Specter Island! Bob mentioned that on the drive in. How was it named?" she asked her.

"I'm not sure; it has some folk lore, but it's just an island like any other. Some people like to stop there and have a picnic. If you stop, you'll have to get your kayak back in the water on your own."

"I think we can handle that. I used to kayak here every summer." Bob told her.

"Sounds good. Ready?"

"Ready!" Cari called out. Bob seemed a bit distracted but gave Dale a nod.

Dale pushed the kayak into the lake. Cari looked to her left and saw that Rich was already zipping himself into a single. She hadn't even seen him walk away. She put her paddle into the water on the right side and started lightly stroking.

"You stay on the right side and I'll do the left. Hopefully, we'll be fairly equal in our strength." Bob directed her.

"Aye, aye, Captain!" Cari called out to him.

The breeze coming off the lake was refreshing. Cari looked around and couldn't believe she was really kayaking on Lake Superior. It felt so peaceful.

"This is amazing, Bob! I love it."

"It's pretty incredible. It shouldn't take us too long to get to the first set of caves, if I remember it correctly. We just need to stay to the lefthand side."

They gradually worked their way to an outcropping of rocks. While the shoreline where they had entered the lake was sandy, like an ocean beach, the edge of the lake to their left had high rock walls. She could hear the water crashing into them as they floated along.

"Okay, I'm going to paddle on the right now too and we'll turn to the left," Bob said from behind her.

The kayak made a gentle left turn as they drifted past the first rock peninsula. Cari looked at the shore and saw two openings along the wall of rocks.

"Oh wow! There really are caves!" she exclaimed.

"Did you think I was lying?" he teased her.

"Well, no, but I didn't think they would be this big. I think the kayak would fit inside the second one."

"Oh, it definitely will. Do you want to try it?"

"You know I do!"

They paddled their way over to the second cave and slowly entered. The ceiling was high enough that they didn't need to duck. The opening of the cave was so large that some sunlight got in, but Cari still needed a moment for her eyes to adjust to the darker conditions.

"Wow! It's incredible. What a neat little cave! Let's take a photo. I'll get my phone out."

"Don't drop it in the lake. We'll never find it."

"Ha ha. I'll do my best."

She wiggled her phone out from the zippered pocket and then carefully removed it from the plastic bag. After unlocking it, she selected the camera app. The flash was already on.

"Ready for a selfie?" she asked Bob.

"Cheese," he replied.

She held the phone up and positioned it so they were both in the photo. In the dim light, it was kind of hard to see what else she would get in the picture. She clicked the white button anyway and the bright light blinded both of them for a moment. She looked at the result and smiled. You could see the edge of the opening just over Bob's shoulder.

"It turned out great. Where to next?"

"Let's get turned around and then head along the shore line further. There are a few more caves I want to show you."

They maneuvered the kayak around the cave until it was facing the lake again. The kayak rocked a bit. Cari looked back to see what Bob was doing.

"Everything okay back there?"

Bob had twisted around in his seat and was starting to open the bulkhead behind his seat. "I was just going to grab a bottle of water, but maybe I should wait until we stop. I don't want to tip us over."

"Are you sure? We don't want to get dehydrated."

"I'm fine. It will only take another thirty minutes or so to get there."

"How far is it to Specter Island?"

"That's probably another hour past the next stop. Feel up for it?"

"Definitely! This is amazing."

"Okay, let's get back to paddling."

Cari followed Bob's direction and paddled mostly on the right side unless they started veering too far left. She knew they needed to be careful not to drift out to the middle of the lake. They could get stranded out there and have to call for help.

The kayak floated easily across the surface of the lake. Cari always knew when Bob was switching sides with his paddle as water would drip down her back as he moved it over. Luckily, it wasn't cold out. She watched the shoreline as they passed several more areas where the rock wall jutted into the lake. Bob seemed extra quiet today. She wondered what was on his mind.

"Whatcha thinking?" she called out over her shoulder.

After a few moments, Bob finally responded. "I'm sorry. Did you ask me something?"

"I was just wondering what was on your mind. You've seemed preoccupied today."

"Oh, sorry. I was just thinking…about Aunt Lydia. I hope everything is working out with the sheriff."

"Me too. I'm sure the break-ins have really rattled her."

"I think we're almost to the cave I wanted to show you."

"Cool. Should we try to drift more to the left?"

"Let me just look around this next bend."

They continued a bit further and Cari looked at the rock face to her left. She couldn't see any caves and wondered if there was a hidden bend she couldn't see. She heard Bob sigh.

"Is this not the right one?"

"No, I thought we would be there by now, but maybe I was misremembering my childhood. It must be the next one. Stay the course for now."

* * * * *

"Hi, Sheriff Maruthers. Thank you so much for calling. I really appreciate it."

"Not a problem, Ms., uh, I don't think I caught your last name." The sheriff's contralto voice rang with assertiveness through the phone.

"It's Fairchild. Lydia Fairchild. Please, just call me Lydia. Everyone does."

"Okay, then Lydia. I understand you've been having some break-ins at your business."

"Yes, ma'am, uh, Sheriff. I have filed a report, but I don't think it's deterring anyone."

"I'm going to come down there with a deputy after we get off the phone. We'll want to see if the burglar left any evidence during the break-in this morning. Why don't you tell me about all the break-ins first?"

"Okay. Let's see. Until this morning, they've all happened in the middle of the night. Twice, they broke windows to get in. A few nights ago, they were able to get in the back door and enter the basement."

"Has anything been stolen?"

"Not that I can tell. I noticed some of my old guest registration books were tossed on the floor. It's possible one of those went missing. Though, for the life of me, I don't know what someone would want with one of those."

"You said that you've filed reports for these other break-ins. Was that with my department or someone else?"

"You're going to think I'm an idiot, but I just don't know. I probably called your department. I guess. It could have been the state police though, or maybe it was the PD from the next town over, uh, Danison. I'm sorry if I've made a mess of things."

"I'll check with Danison. They may have sent someone out. Don't you worry, Lydia. We're going to figure out who's doing this and put a stop to it. Now, your address is 301 East Lake Drive in Harborville, correct?"

"That's correct."

"I pulled up the address and we don't have any reports of break-ins in our system, so you must have spoken with Danison PD. I'll make a note to get information from them to add to our own file. I'm sure they'll be happy to turn the case over to us."

"Thank you, Sheriff."

"My deputy and I will be over there in twenty to thirty minutes."

"Okay, thank you again, Sheriff."

Lydia hung up the phone and wrung her hands. She felt like a fool for not keeping track of the police reports. She just wanted it all to go away. At least the business was full this week. So many guests had canceled their trips since the break-ins started. If she couldn't put a stop to it soon, she would be out of business.

* * * * *

Lydia watched from the window of her office for the sheriff's cruiser to arrive. She had already checked on the breakfast crowd and made sure everything was running smoothly for the day. Her hands twisted in her lap and her foot tapped out a nervous rhythm as she continued to stare out the window. She didn't have a clue why someone kept breaking into The Boarding House, but she hoped the sheriff could help.

After Bob and Cari left, she typed up an email to send to each of the current guests, informing them of another break-in. She checked her guests' history and was relieved to see none of her current guests had been at the house for the previous break-in. Lydia checked her watch: it was just after ten a.m., so she felt comfortable making a call to each room. She took a deep breath and picked up the landline.

The guest in room one answered on the third ring. "Hello?"

"Hello, Mr. Chaswick, this is Lydia with the Boarding House—"

"Oh, you just sent an email."

"Yes, and I wanted to call to make sure you received it."

"About the break-in? Was anyone hurt? I mean, your email said no one was hurt and nothing was stolen and the police were investigating, but was the guy armed or...?" the man finally paused in his ramblings.

"Oh no. The intruder was not armed, nor did anyone get hurt. The county sheriff is on her way here to investigate. Um, did you have any other questions?" Lydia almost didn't ask after his last verbal release.

"I guess not. I mean, this is one of the safest counties in the US, right?"

"I, uh, is it?" Lydia stuttered.

"Yeah, I Googled it after I got your email. It's seventh on the list of low crime places."

"Well, that's good to know. If you have any questions, please don't hesitate to ask. Thank you again for choosing us for your vacation."

"Cool. See ya around." He ended the call.

Lydia scrunched her eyebrows in confusion. She expected most guests to be concerned about a break-in, but Mr. Chaswick had almost seemed flippant about it. Maybe the other guests wouldn't pack their bags and leave either. She dialed the next room on the list, but no one answered. She left a voicemail, which would make the light on the phone blink. *Hopefully, they'll see it.* She checked her records for the next occupied room and dialed the number. She thought she was going to have to leave another message when an out-of-breath voice came on the line.

"Hello?" the woman's voice breathed into the phone.

"Is this Ms. Venaci?"

"Yes, yes. Is this the front desk? Is something wrong?" she sounded panicked.

Lydia tried to keep her voice calm and even. "I'm calling to verify you received my email."

"About the break-in? Did they come back? Do we need to evacuate? I've been a nervous wreck since I read your email. Oh dear."

Lydia cringed. She didn't want to frighten anyone, but she also didn't want to lose business. "Yes, about the break-in. No, no one has come back. There's no need for alarm. The sheriff is on her way to investigate, but it was not an armed intruder and no one was hurt."

"Yes, yes, you said that in the email. Oh dear. Oh dear." the woman kept repeating the phrase with more and more urgency. "My kids told me not to worry about it. I'm safe. Break-ins happen. They convinced me to come here to relax. I've been so anxious since my poor Buddy died and they thought if I got out of the house…"

"I'm sorry to interrupt; who is Buddy?"

"Buddy was my pet beagle. He was the best dog you could ask for. He went with me everywhere. He was my guard dog, and my best friend. I know it's silly to say he was a guard dog when he wasn't that big, but he kept me safe…"

The woman droned on and on about her beloved dog. Lydia felt like she had to listen, but also needed to call the other rooms. She drummed her fingers quietly on her thigh.

"...Anyway, my kids thought if I got out of the house and got pampered for a few days, I would be able to relax, but oh dear! This was not expected. I'm not sure what to do."

"Have you had breakfast yet, Ms. Venaci?" Lydia asked her.

"Um, no, I've been pacing back and forth in my room. Is it too late for breakfast?"

"No, ma'am. Not at all. How about I send something to your room? Do you prefer coffee or tea?"

"Oh, that would be lovely. I don't drink coffee. It's too much for my nerves. I would love some chamomile tea and a scone—do you have scones?"

"Certainly. Let me just call over to the kitchen and someone will bring it by in the next ten minutes or so. On the house."

"Oh, thank you so much."

"If you need anything else, please come by my office or the front desk. I hope you enjoy the rest of your stay."

Lydia ended the call and quickly phoned the kitchen to get the tea and a scone ordered for Ms. Venaci. She hoped the woman would be able to calm down and enjoy her time away from home. It was kind of her children to try to help their mother relax.

She dialed the final two rooms on her list and was relieved to be able to just leave a message for both rooms. So far, no one had come by the office to request a refund on the remainder of their stay. She hoped she wouldn't lose any more customers. Just as she was about to give up on the sheriff and go busy herself with another task, a large, brown sedan rounded the corner and parked along the curb. "Lake County Sheriff" was painted along the body of the vehicle.

The passenger door opened revealing a young, white man who looked to be around Bob and Cari's age. He had brown hair and a muscular frame. The man was an inch or two shorter than Sheriff Maruthers and carried a metal case. The sheriff's brown curls framed her dark, angular face. She walked with confidence up the steps to the bed and breakfast. Lydia rushed to greet them at the door.

"Sheriff Maruthers! Thank you so much for making the trip out," Lydia shook her hand as she guided the two law enforcement people inside.

"Not a problem, ma'am. This is my deputy, Stephen Yarrow." She nodded at Yarrow to introduce himself.

"Deputy Yarrow, ma'am," he said as he shook her hand.

"Lydia. Lydia Fairchild, but please, call me Lydia. My office is right over here."

They followed her through the open door and took the seats previously occupied by Bob and Cari. Deputy Yarrow pulled out a small notebook and pencil. They both sat on the edge of their chairs.

"Why don't you start by telling us about the break-in today?" Sheriff Maruthers requested.

"Okay. Let's see. My guests in one of the third-floor suites got up earlier this morning to exercise. When one of them returned to the room about half an hour later, she noticed the door was not quite closed. She called out before entering the room and the door was pushed back into her face. That's when she knew someone was in there who shouldn't be. By the time she entered the room, the man was already out on the balcony and climbing over the railing."

"Can we speak with the guest? Did she get a good look at the man?" Yarrow asked her.

"Oh, I didn't realize you'd want to interview her. I feel ridiculous for telling her it was fine to leave. She'll be back later this afternoon."

"Did she say if she got a good look at the man?"

"Oh, no. She could only see him from the back."

"Why don't you ask her to give us a call when she returns? We can ask her for any distinguishing features and anything else she remembers." Sheriff Maruthers requested.

"I can do that."

"You mentioned on the phone that you've had more than one break-in over the last month. How many?"

Lydia dipped her head before responding, her cheeks red in embarrassment. "Counting this morning, there have been four."

"And you don't think anything has been stolen so far?" Yarrow asked her.

"I can't say that with one hundred percent confidence. The intruder in the basement last week...he dumped several of my old guestbooks onto the floor. It's possible he took one."

"You say 'he'. Are you certain it was a man? I was under the impression you didn't have any video set up here." Yarrow questioned her further.

"Oh, sorry. I don't know the gender of the intruder. I was just making an assumption. Until today, no one has seen the person breaking in. I suppose it could have been a different person each time. I just have a feeling it's one person and they're searching for something. For the life of me, I can't figure out what it could be."

"Let's go down to the basement and see what we can find," Sheriff Maruthers said. "Deputy Yarrow, you go up to three and dust for prints."

"Oh, you'll need the key for that. My guests' things are still in there, but they are out kayaking today. They gave me permission for you to enter the room and investigate." Lydia told him as she pulled a key from a board on the wall behind her.

Both Yarrow and Maruthers raised their eyebrows in surprise.

"Well, you see, my nephew and his, uh, girlfriend are staying in that room. They wanted to stay and help me speak with you, but I didn't want to ruin their vacation any more than I already have." Lydia explained. "Here's the key to their room. It's number nine."

Deputy Yarrow took the key with the plastic keychain from her. The number 9 was imprinted onto the red plastic. He put it in his shirt pocket and stood up.

"Let me grab a fingerprint kit from you before you go upstairs, deputy," the sheriff requested.

Yarrow picked up the metal case and set it on the desk. He popped the clasps open and handed a plastic, resealable bag to Sheriff Maruthers. She took it and stood up.

"Let's see what we can find. Hopefully, this guy left a few prints behind. Lydia, lead the way. You can tell me more about the other break-ins while I dust for prints."

* * * * *

Cari wiped sweat from her forehead and rolled her head around to ease some tension. They were closing in on Specter Island now, but still hadn't found the cave Bob was hoping to show her. She could tell he was getting frustrated but hoped he realized she was still enjoying the excursion.

"Maybe we should just go over to Specter Island and try to find the cave on the way back," she suggested.

"I'm sorry, Cari. I can't believe I missed it. It was our favorite cave to explore with the kayaks when I was growing up. We would always head right to it. I thought for sure I could find it again."

"Look! There's a cave. It looks enormous. Is that it?" Cari pointed at another opening in the rock face.

"I don't think so. The other one is different; I should have brought photos. Then you could have helped me look for it too."

"Can we check this one out?"

"Sure. Might as well."

They turned the kayak towards the cave and paddled over to it. The cave's entrance was even larger than the previous one. Cari pulled out her phone and turned on the flashlight feature.

"Look, Bob. The cave walls are covered in drawings! Do you see them?"

"I do. I don't think I've been in this cave before."

"Look over there," Cari shined the flashlight to her right. "It looks like someone has been digging or something."

"It does. Who would dig inside a cave?" he wondered aloud.

"Maybe there's a treasure buried in here!"

Bob snorted. "No way. These caves have been here for ages and people are constantly going in and out of them. No one could secretly stash some sort of treasure."

"Well, someone is looking for something," she told him.

Cari took her phone out of its little bag again and snapped some photos of the drawings and the place where someone had been digging. She didn't see any tools, but there wasn't really a surface to leave them on. The hole in the cave wall was about the size of a man's head, but more oval-shaped. She heard her stomach rumble and realized they hadn't had anything to eat since breakfast.

"Are you getting hungry? My stomach is rumbling."

"It's getting close to one o'clock. You must be starving! I'm sorry, Cari," Bob apologized.

"Bob, I'm not *that* hungry yet. You said you had some snacks, right?"

"Yeah, I…I have some things. Just a sec."

Cari could hear the disappointment in his voice and wanted to reassure him that the day wasn't a failure. "Do we still have time to make it to Specter Island?"

"I'm not sure. It seems like the wind is more of a crosswind now, so it won't help push us home. We might need to just eat in the kayak and turn around."

"Works for me. Hand me one of those granola bars."

"Uh, I actually have something more than granola bars. Let's get out of the cave and then I can see what I'm doing better."

They turned the kayak again and paddled their way back to the open water. Cari felt the kayak rock a bit when Bob pulled his backpack out.

"Here's a sandwich," he said as he passed a neatly wrapped package up to her. "And here's a bottle of water."

Cari turned around and looked at him. "Did you pack a whole picnic in there?"

He blushed. "Aunt Lydia put some things together for us."

Cari unwrapped her sandwich and took a bite. "This is delicious. What's in it?"

"I'm not sure. She told me she asked the chef to put a picnic lunch together for me."

"That's so sweet. A picnic would have been fun, but this is nice too. How is your sandwich?"

"Pretty tasty, but then, hunger is a tasty sauce."

Cari laughed. "That it is."

"I think we have some fruit and some kind of dessert or cookie too."

"Pass it on up!"

They ate in silence. Cari wanted to take more photos but didn't think she could balance the sandwich, fruit, and her phone at the same time. She had the bottle of water in her lap.

"Maybe we could come back tomorrow. I'd like to get another look in that cave and see some more of the drawings. Is it legal for someone to dig in these caves? Should we report that to someone?"

"I'm not sure. We can ask Aunt Lydia when we get back. And I'd love to come out again tomorrow. We'll head straight for this cave and then go over to Specter Island. I really want you to get to see that."

"It's a date." She turned and winked at him, which rocked the kayak a bit.

"Woah. Careful…"

"Sorry!" She giggled.

"I'll take your trash if you're ready to head back."

Cari passed the sandwich wrapper and empty fruit container back to Bob. He stuffed it into the backpack while she took another swig of water before handing it back too.

"Ready to get back to shore?"

"Let's do it."

Chapter 6

ydia watched as Sheriff Maruthers brushed fingerprint powder onto various surfaces. The sheriff had told her they would need to collect elimination prints from her and her staff. Luckily, they had a digital print scanner, so no one would have to worry about getting ink off their fingers or hands. The sheriff was focused on pulling what looked like palm prints from the crossbar on the exit door. The bar had to be depressed for someone to get it opened.

"I found a few prints over here. How often is this door used? It looks like an emergency exit, right?" She asked Lydia.

"It's almost never used, though I did go through it when I heard the intruder down here just recently." Lydia responded.

"I assume the other side has a lever and a handle. You would have used that to come back in, correct?"

"I did. I guess you're saying I wiped their print off the lever when I re-entered?"

Sheriff Maruthers nodded. "Most likely, though, you don't know they came in from that door."

"I keep the interior door to the basement locked from around ten o'clock at night to eight the next morning. It used to stay unlocked all day, but we were getting lots of complaints about loud guests when others were trying to sleep. Also, I noticed some scrapes along the door jamb when I came down. I thought the intruder might have used a crowbar to get in here."

The sheriff nodded. She photographed the palm prints on the push bar and then lifted them with tape. She carefully pushed the door open with her gloved hands and inspected the jam.

"You're right. It seems like they pried their way in right here," she pointed at the scratches along the wood frame. "I found a few partial prints over on the bookshelf where you keep the old guest registries. Why don't you go through the books and see if they're all there?"

Lydia crossed the room to the bookshelf and pulled a few off the shelf. The ones on the lower shelf hadn't been disturbed. The newer registries had dates listed on the binding, which made it easier to keep them in order. She hadn't gone back to write the dates on the older volumes yet, so she had to flip each one open to look. The covers of the registries from the first few decades were made from starched cloth stretched over cardboard. The pale-yellow books were slightly thinner than the more modern-made books. Lydia and Harvey had purchased plastic covers for the old books to help preserve them. She began sorting the old registries by date to get them back in order. Her shoulders slumped when she realized one was missing after all.

"What is it?"

"The oldest guestbook. It's gone. I guess something has been stolen. It doesn't really have any value, but it was kind of fun to say we had signatures from all those years ago."

"Why would someone take it?"

"I haven't the foggiest. I'm certain it's worthless."

Lydia pushed herself off the floor and stood up. Sheriff Maruthers made a few more notes before sliding her small notebook back into her pocket. They both looked toward the stairs when they heard the interior door creak open.

"It's just me," Deputy Yarrow called out as he made his way down the stairs. "I pulled a few prints from the balcony up on the third floor. We'll need to get your guests' prints from that room too."

"Should I send them to your office? They are supposed to be back later this afternoon, but I can call them if you need them sooner."

"Why don't you have them give us a call when they return? We're going to get these prints scanned in and sorted. We'll eliminate you and your staff, then see if we get any hits in the databases we have access to."

"Okay. Can you collect our prints with your tablet in my office? I can send my staff members over one by one," she paused. "I almost forgot. One of my guests a couple weeks ago woke up when the dining room window shattered. He helped me clean it up. Should I contact him and have him submit his prints too?"

"First question, yes, we can use your office to print you and your staff. Second question: no. More than likely, his prints are long gone." Sheriff Maruthers told her. "Do you have any more questions for us?"

"Well, would you be able to recommend a security company to me? I'm worried it won't be in my budget, but if people keep breaking in, I'll lose my business entirely."

"I can't make referrals because of potential conflicts of interest, but there are several reputable companies in the area. Check the reviews online. You'll quickly see who is trustworthy."

"Thank you. That's next on my list today. Let me get you set up in my office, and then I'll start sending my staff over."

The two officers followed Lydia up the stairs. It was only one o'clock, but she could feel the weariness in her steps. She tried to remain optimistic. The police officers seemed competent and had found some promising prints. Of course, they could be hers or her staff's. The restaurant would almost be finished with the lunch crowd and the rest of her staff was still on-site changing bedding, cleaning rooms, and prepping for dinner. She let the officers back into her office and went to instruct her staff to get their hands scanned.

* * * * *

A man peered out from the cave opening and watched as the two-person kayak continued along the lake. He had watched them from the shadows and overheard their plans to return the next day to explore more caves. Thankfully, they hadn't seen him when they looked around this particular cave. He knew the woman saw the hole he'd dug into the wall. Most kayakers didn't make it out this far, so he thought he would have the place to himself.

He used his paddle to push his kayak back into the cave. The couple hadn't seen the extra compartment to the cave, so he had been able to hide in the back crevice while they shone a light around the interior. He pulled the small metal detector from the fasteners holding it to his shoulders. The first place the device had beeped was where he had already dug a foot into the cave wall. Normally, he took time to fill in the places he dug, but the couple had startled him, forcing him to hide before he was discovered. He turned on his headlamp and peered into the hole again. It was still empty. He slowly waved the detector over it. He cursed under his breath; the device remained silent. Whatever triggered it before was gone. He scanned more of the cave wall and still didn't pick up anything.

He cursed again. He had to fill in the hole and then finish scanning the cave. He pulled a journal from his vest and used the attached pen to put a star next to the cave. He wished he knew how deep into the cave wall he needed to dig. If only he could find the original map! Then he could get the treasure and stop lurking through these caves. He reattached the detector to his shoulders, then reached forward to pull a small, waterproof bag from the bulkhead. It had all the debris he'd cleared from the hole as well as a little plaster to hold it in place. He carefully pushed the rocks and pebbles into the opening and then smeared a little plaster over the pile to seal them in tight. Then he pushed the remaining rocks into the goo, trying to mirror the surfaces next to his hole. Maybe the metal detector had picked up the iron in the rocks. He had no idea; he wasn't a geologist.

The man still had time to search the cave. He retrieved the detector and started working his way around the space. It was too large to effectively search all of it in one day and he was worried the couple might return to look around again the next day. He'd have to come back tomorrow and find a way to scare them off. Most people were satisfied to just nose their kayaks into the caves and do a quick look-around, but he had seen the curiosity in the woman's eyes. She wasn't just sightseeing. She was looking for more.

* * * * *

Bob grimaced as he paddled from the back of the kayak. The day had not gone at all as he envisioned it. Between the burglar, the apparent wild-goose-chase to find his favorite childhood cave, and this missed picnic, he couldn't have been more frustrated. He knew Cari was picking up on his mood and felt bad for not enjoying his time with her.

He had double- and triple-checked the backpack for the little ring box every time he got something out of it. He'd felt his heart drop into his stomach when he realized their room had been broken into that morning. He wasn't going to leave the ring behind again.

When he told his parents he was planning to propose to Cari, his mom had suggested taking a romantic trip and visiting the family bed and breakfast. Cari wasn't a hopeless romantic, but he had planned to propose during a lakeside picnic in the middle of the kayak trip. They needed to return the kayak by three o'clock, so they were having to really work to get back to the shore where they started. His arms were sore and he was almost dreading coming back the next day. He could tell Cari was excited and hoped he wasn't being too much of a downer. He realized she was talking to him again and shook his head to regain focus. Between the crosswind and her facing away from him, he had a hard time hearing what she was saying.

"I'm sorry, what?"

"You seem pretty distracted still. Is everything okay? Did you hear from Lydia?"

"I'm sorry. No, I haven't heard from her, but I might not hear my phone through this vest and the plastic bag."

"Should we check? What if she has questions for us?"

"We're almost back to shore. It shouldn't take more than another half hour or so. I can see the shoreline."

"Are you at least having fun?"

"I am. It's great to see you enjoying the lake."

"It's so beautiful…and fascinating. I love it!" She called out from the front seat.

He smiled. "I can tell. I'm glad it's been a fun day even though it started out a little rough."

She turned her head and smiled back at him, rocking the kayak a bit.

"Whoops! Sorry. Guess I'll keep facing forward and paddling on the right."

They slipped back into silence and continued towards the shore. Bob was ready to get back to the bed and breakfast. He needed to reconfigure his proposal plans now.

He mirrored Cari's rhythm with her paddle and they glided across the lake towards their destination. He could see Dale and

Rich on the beach waving at them. He hoped they weren't too annoyed with him. He checked his watch again. They weren't late, yet, but it was getting close.

* * * * *

Cari unstrapped her life jacket and handed it back to Rich. Bob's shoulders slumped as he watched Dale dragging the kayak back to the nearby trees. She wondered why he was so disappointed about one cave.

"You said you wanted to come back out tomorrow?" Dale asked Bob.

"Do you have space for us to take a double out again?"

Dale pulled out her phone and scrolled through a few screens. "I do. What time will you be here?"

Bob looked at Cari. "I can be ready at the same time," she told him.

"How about ten o'clock?" Bob asked.

"Until three again?" Dale asked as she made a note in her phone.

"Yes, ma'am. Thank you."

"Okay then. See you tomorrow."

Cari and Bob retraced their steps from that morning back to the rental car. She could feel Bob's frustrations as he stomped along the path. She reached over and grabbed his hand and pulled him into a hug.

After a quick kiss, Cari said, "This was fun, Bob. Thank you for giving me a tour of this side of the lake."

"I'm sorry I got so lost. I ruined the picnic."

"Hey, we still got to eat, right?"

He gave her a small smile and a responding kiss. "We did. I have a dinner reservation at a local restaurant tonight. More seafood specials, but they'll have other entrees too."

"I'm sure it will be amazing. I am going to need another shower after the kayak workout, though."

* * * * *

"Okay, Lydia, I think that's everyone. It will take us some time to get through these prints. In the meantime, we will step up patrols through Harborville in an effort to deter your intruder."

Lydia bit her lip. "I don't want to be a burden."

"It's no burden. I strongly encourage you to get someone out here ASAP to install a security system. Video monitoring would be a big help."

"It's next on my list after I make sure the dinner staff is ready to go. Let me show you out."

Lydia accompanied Sheriff Maruthers and Deputy Yarrow to the front door. Just as they reached the sidewalk, Bob and Cari strolled up from the parking lot looking worn out.

"Sheriff!" Lydia called out.

Sheriff Maruthers turned on her heel. "Yes, ma'am?"

"This is my nephew and…this is the couple whose room was broken into." She gestured towards Bob and Cari.

"Oh, perfect timing! We just need to steal a moment of your time." Deputy Yarrow told them.

"Of course. How can we help?" Cari asked not noticing Lydia's concerned expression.

Bob looked at Lydia and sighed, then turned to the police officers. "Certainly."

Lydia decided she didn't need to eavesdrop and went back to her office to lock the door. She patted the front of her pants to check that her ring of keys was still latched to her belt loop and then headed for the kitchen. Besides Bob and Cari, none of her guests had returned to the house from their activities yet. She was relieved no one had requested an early termination of their stay.

She wondered how Ms. Venaci was holding up. Maybe no news was good news.

The kitchen was a blur of activity. Servers were rolling silverware into napkins and placing them into glasses so the tables could be set. Her head chef was barking orders to the other cook, who was chopping onions on a cutting board. Rather than disrupt their coordinated chaos, she just nodded and turned back to her office.

The landline was ringing as she unlocked her office door. She crossed the room quickly and answered it. She crossed her fingers and hoped it wasn't Ms. Venaci asking for a refund.

"The Boarding House, this is Lydia. How can I help you today?" She said cautiously.

"My name is Rick Patella, like the knee cap. I'm a realtor in your area and wondered if you would be interested in selling your property at 301 East Lake Drive?"

Lydia was taken aback. "Absolutely not!"

"It's a seller's market. I'm sure I could get you a great price on the property. I have a potential buyer already asking about it."

"Mr., uh, Patella, I am not interested in selling."

"Don't you even want to hear what they're offering? I believe it to be a generous offer...considering."

"Considering what?" Lydia asked with concern.

"Oh, nothing nefarious, just the usual. Market value, square footage, comparable sales in the area."

"What sales in the area?" she asked, starting to get annoyed.

"I have a list. Do you have a realtor? I would be happy to recommend one as representing you myself would be a bit of a conflict of interest. You understand."

"I don't think I do," she said darkly.

"I'm going to drop this offer by your office later today. You look it over and call me with any questions. I look forward to hearing from you."

The call ended. Lydia stood with the receiver in her hand trying to process what the man had said. Her business wasn't for sale, so who thought they could try to buy it?

* * * * *

Cari pressed her finger onto the deputy's screen. It instructed her to roll the pad of her finger across the surface from various directions so the device could get an accurate scan of her entire print. It took longer than just inking her fingers, but she had been relieved to hear she didn't need to get ink all over her hands to have her prints taken.

"Okay, that's all your fingerprints. Let's get your palms now, Ms. Turnlyle," Deputy Yarrow requested after selecting a new setting in the app.

"Please, call me Cari. Do I just place my whole hand on the screen?"

"It will be a similar process to your fingerprints. Just follow the instructions again."

She rolled her palm on the screen's surface, then stretched her fingers to flatten it. Eventually, the device was satisfied it had scanned her entire palm and instructed her to switch hands. Cari watched Bob from the corner of her eye. He was fidgeting with the backpack straps. She knew the break-in had really rattled him and not just because she was the one to startle the intruder.

"Okay, Ms., uh, Cari. You're all set. Sheriff Maruthers has a few questions for you while I get Mr. Hursley's prints. Mr. Hursley?" Deputy Yarrow waved Bob over.

Sheriff Maruthers was leaning against the hood of her cruiser. Cari felt a bit odd giving a statement outside rather than in an office, but it seemed like they were almost finished. The sheriff smiled when Cari stepped towards her.

"Ms. Turnlyle, right?" The sheriff extended her hand.

"Cari is fine, thanks," she politely said as she shook the woman's hand.

"Cari it is. I'm Sheriff Maruthers. Can you walk me through your encounter with the intruder? You are certain the door was locked?"

"Yes. Bob, uh, my boyfriend..." she gestured towards Bob. "Bob is very careful about locking doors and being safe. He's actually a crime scene tech where we live in New York."

"Really? How interesting. Okay, so you returned to your room and the door was not closed?"

"Right. That kind of set me on edge."

Cari told the sheriff the rest of her encounter, including how he knocked into her with the door first. The sheriff listened intently and wrote a few things down in a small notebook. When she finished, Sheriff Maruthers clicked her pen closed and stuck it back into her front shirt pocket.

"Thank you, Cari. Hopefully, one of the prints Deputy Yarrow or I pulled can be used to track him down. If you think of anything else, please don't hesitate to give us a call." She handed her a business card.

"Thank you, sheriff," Cari said as she stuck the card into her pocket.

"Yarrow, are you about finished up?" She looked at her deputy.

"One more scan and I think we're there," the younger man responded.

Bob lifted his palm off the screen and looked expectantly at the deputy. He clicked through a few prompts and then turned the screen off.

"Great. Thank you for your time and helpfulness. Mr. Hursley, please let your aunt know that we will give her a call after we've run all these prints."

"Of course. Thank you for your thoroughness." Bob shook his hand.

74

The two officers got back into the cruiser. Cari walked over to Bob as the vehicle pulled away from the curb. He was bouncing on his toes a bit.

"Are you sure you're okay?"

"I'm fine. I'm sorry for being so distracted today." He looked at his watch. "It's closing in on four o'clock. Why don't we each get cleaned up and then we can go for another pre-dinner walk?"

She smiled at him. "Sounds lovely."

"I just need to check in with Aunt Lydia, then I'll be right up."

They parted ways at the staircase. Cari squeezed Bob's hand before climbing the stairs to their room. She hoped he would be back to himself soon.

* * * * *

Lydia opened her internet browser to search for security companies in the area. The list of results spanned several pages. Her shoulders drooped as she let out an exasperated sigh. Sheriff Maruthers recommended she look at the customer reviews before deciding on a company. She scanned the list of results. The first few were sponsored by the search engine, but as she scrolled down the page, she saw the familiar rows of five small stars. She started to click on one with a 4.8-star rating when a knock at the door made her jump.

"Just a moment," she called out.

"Aunt Lydia, it's me," Bob responded.

"Oh, Bob! Come on in."

Bob opened the door and sat his backpack down in one of the empty chairs. He kept his hand on it as he sat down in the other chair. She noticed his left knee was bouncing rapidly.

"Is everything okay?" She looked at the backpack. "Did the proposal not go well?"

Bob sighed and ran his thumb along one of the straps. "I never got the chance to ask. We got turned around a bit, well, I did. Then, it was too late to do the picnic, so we had to kind of wing it in the kayak. I didn't want to get the ring out while we were over the water, of course."

"Oh, of course! That could have been a disaster."

He sighed again. "It sure felt like one anyway."

"It's only your first full day here. Don't worry."

He cleared his throat. "How did everything go with the sheriff? Do you feel confident they'll make this a priority?"

"I think it went very well. She suggested I check out customer reviews of security companies before asking for quotes, so that's what I was starting to do. It's a pretty long list."

"Can I take a look?"

Lydia hesitated. Bob was supposed to be on vacation. "Well…"

"I might see one I'm familiar with. It will just take a second." He got up and walked around the desk. "Don't just look at the review ratings. Some of them might only have a handful of reviews and they could have all been submitted by friends or family members who may or may not use the company."

"Oh, I didn't even think of that! This one has over a thousand and a high rating. What do you think?"

She watched Bob's face as he stared at the computer screen, reading the list of companies. He lifted his hand and started to reach for her mouse, but stopped short.

"It looks like there are two or three with pretty high ratings near the top with a good number of reviews. Read through some of the negative ones too. See if everyone has the same problem, or if it's just people complaining about something less than perfection."

"Good advice. Thank you, Bob. So, do you recognize any of these?"

He frowned. "I don't. I'm sure some of the big-name places are out here too, but you should also look at some of the more locally owned ones. Let me read some of the reviews. Is it okay if I take over here for a minute?"

"Certainly," she moved out of his way and he expanded the reviews for the first company on the list.

She watched as he scrolled through the users' reviews, switching over to the one- and two-star ratings. The text on the screen was moving faster than she could read it, so she looked away. She tried to wait patiently while Bob clicked through the search results for several minutes. He must have sensed her impatience and looked up.

"See, like this company, for example," he motioned her closer to the computer. "They have a pretty high overall rating, but when you read the negative reviews, they're very similar: *I have to constantly replace the camera battery. Every other week. I was told it was hard-wired into the building, but it shuts off every two weeks,*" he read from the screen.

"And that's followed by a different user saying basically the same thing about the batteries. All of the negative reviews address that issue, which tells you it's a common problem, not just user error."

Lydia made a note of the company and Bob went back to clicking through the results. Part of her wanted him to just say which company she should use and part of her felt guilty for taking him away from his vacation. She chewed on the inside of her cheek and fiddled with her apron strings for a few minutes before speaking again.

"Find anything promising?" she asked with her eyebrows raised.

He shrugged. "I mean, there are a lot of good companies here. I would pick a few and ask for quotes, then you can decide what best fits your needs."

"You make it sound so easy. Hopefully, I can get one selected and have the system installed easily."

Bob got up to exit her office and almost ran into another man on his way out. Lydia smiled at first, thinking he might be a new guest. She didn't think anyone was checking in today, but maybe it had slipped her mind. She was just about to greet him when she saw the manilla envelope in his hand.

"Ms. Fairchild?"

"Yes..." she said slowly.

"I'm a courier for Blankenship and Patella Realty. Here's the offer Mr. Patella mentioned to you over the phone. He said to tell you he hopes you'll give it serious consideration. Also, his card is in there if you want to call his office to get your own realtor."

She felt the color draining from her face and took a quick look at Bob. His jaw dropped and then snapped closed as she took the envelope from the man. She hadn't wanted anyone to know about the offer. It was ludicrous that someone was trying to buy her business! The realtor left her office as quickly as he'd entered it. Bob shifted his weight from foot to foot; his bewildered look left Lydia stumbling for words.

"It's not what you think, Bob. I can explain. It's...it's..." she stuttered.

"It's...none of my business."

He picked up the backpack and started to leave the office when Cari walked in. Lydia swallowed and tried to regain her composure. This day was getting worse and worse by the minute.

"Cari! I'm sorry. I got caught up with—"

"Is everything okay? You both look like you're in shock." Cari interrupted Bob.

"Everything is fine." Lydia lied. "An unexpected visitor just stopped by. He, um, he's, well...oh dear. Why don't you both have a seat? I'll try to explain.

"A realtor contacted me about a buyer interested in the bed and breakfast. He called yesterday and again today. And before you ask, *no*, the business is *not for sale*. I'm not sure what instigated his interest, but I have explicitly stated that I'm not interested, but apparently, he's being persistent. Maybe the person has heard about my recent struggles keeping customers after the break-ins." She turned to Bob. "But I would never up and sell this place without talking to everyone first. Yes, I'm the owner and manager, but it's still the family business. I wouldn't spring that on everyone unannounced."

She looked away, afraid to see disappointment on Bob's face. Thoughts raced through her head and rather than react, she straightened the other mail and paperwork on her desk. Their silence seemed to stretch on for minutes, but she knew her anxiety was taking over.

"Aunt Lydia, I'm sorry if you thought my reaction was one of judgment. I was just as shocked as you to have a realtor march in here with an offer for the business. I never once assumed you had it up for sale."

Lydia took a deep breath and willed herself to relax. "Thank you. I'm sorry for being such a mess. Please, you're on vacation. Don't worry about all of this. I'll handle it."

"You can call Dad. He would be happy to help with any of this. Finding a security company, getting the realtor to leave you alone. You don't have to take on the world by yourself, Aunt Lydia."

She nodded. "You're right. I'm being stubborn and it's making me look foolish. I'll speak with your father later. Now, tell me about your kayaking trip. How did it go?"

Cari's face lit up with a smile. "It was absolutely gorgeous. I was just telling my grandmother about it. I got so many good photos. We found this cave. It was big enough to fit our kayak into! When we got inside, it had some drawings on the walls. *And* someone had been digging in it. I don't know what they were looking for, but we're going to go back and take another look."

"And hopefully make it to Specter Island," Bob added.

"Tomorrow?" Lydia asked.

He grinned sheepishly. "Yes, do you think we could get another picnic?"

"Of course! I'll call over to the kitchen right now. It sounds like quite the treasure hunt. You go ahead and enjoy the rest of your day…" she paused. "Oh, by the way, I spoke to Contessa and she hasn't had any break-ins nor has she heard of other businesses in her area having an issue with them. She said to be sure and send you a hello."

Bob ducked his head as his ears went red. Lydia saw Cari's eyes flick his way at the mention of Contessa and wondered if she should have kept the greeting to herself. She started to say something to end the awkward silence when Bob mumbled something that sounded a bit like an 'ok'.

"Thank you, Lydia. We really appreciate you arranging the picnic for us again," Cari said as she grabbed Bob's hand and gave it a squeeze.

She shooed them out of her office for the second time that day. When she was alone, she looked back at the computer screen. The list of security companies stared back at her. She sighed and looked at the rest of the desk. Glaring at the realtor's envelope, she grabbed it. She almost tore it in half but thought better of it. Maybe she could ask Jack to call the realty office and get them to stop harassing her. She lifted the phone receiver and then remembered Bob's request for a picnic. She made that call first, then planned out her conversation with her brother.

* * * * *

"I'm going to take a quick shower, then we can go for the walk I promised you." Bob told Cari.

"Sounds good. I'm going to text these photos to Genevieve. I'll be ready when you are."

Cari watched as Bob started to set his backpack down, but shifted it back onto his shoulder instead. She wondered what made him so possessive of it, but shrugged it off and opened up her messaging app. As she selected photos to send to her friend, her mind wandered back to what happened in Lydia's office. Bob's aunt had clearly been rattled. Between the break-ins and the pesky realtor, she was probably feeling overwhelmed.

She thought back over some of the conversations they'd had with Lydia. She mentioned losing some business because of the break-ins, but hadn't said how much. Cari wondered why Lydia was so hesitant to ask her brother for help. Bob had never mentioned family strife or drama, but she supposed every family had their share of it. And then there was Bob's response to hearing Contessa's name again. She wondered what had transpired between the two of them…and were they still in touch?

"You look deep in thought." Bob's voice startled her back to reality. He had dressed in the bathroom and was pulling his loafers from his suitcase.

She shook Contessa from her head and smiled. "Sorry, I was just thinking about your aunt and everything going on with her business. I wish I could help."

Bob sat down on the bed and pulled on a pair of socks. "She's pretty stubborn. I wish she'd give dad a call."

"Is there some reason she wouldn't?"

"I don't know. I mean, they have always seemed to be competitive with each other. Normal sibling rivalry stuff, you know."

Cari shook her head. "Bea is eight years older than me. We weren't really competitors."

"Still, I'm sure you both wanted to be seen as successful by your parents."

"Sure. I suppose I do compare myself as an adult to Bea as an adult. Do you think Lydia is afraid your dad will see her as a failure if she asks for help? Did he want to be the one who took over the business?"

"I have never heard him say that. He's always been proud of his big sister. Ready to walk?"

"Let's do it. What's the name of the restaurant for tonight?"

"Mel's Superior Seafood."

She smiled. "That's kind of funny, but clever. I'm excited to try it."

They exited the room and made sure the door was locked behind them. Cari led the way down the stairs and out the front door. The air was crisp and a light breeze blew her curls into her face again. She pulled her hair elastic from her wrist and secured her hair into a low ponytail.

"So much for styling my hair."

"It always looks amazing."

She laughed. "You're such a liar."

"I'm not lying," he paused. "Mel's is just a few blocks from here. We actually walked past it last night. We have time to walk along the lake first, though."

Cari grabbed Bob's hand and gave it a squeeze. "I had another question about your aunt and the bed and breakfast."

"Sure, what's up?"

"When we were in her office earlier, she kind of distractedly straightened some papers and envelopes on her desk. One of the pages was a statement from the county tax assessor. Part of it was showing before she gathered everything up. I know I shouldn't have been nosey, but it looked like it had a big increase from last year."

Bob scratched his head with his free hand. "That is interesting. I don't know a lot about the business, but increasing property taxes would definitely add to Lydia's woes."

"Should we ask her about it...or tell your dad?"

Bob bit his lip. "I don't know. I don't really want to betray Aunt Lydia. It's not something we should know about. Let's keep it to ourselves for now and see if she mentions it."

"How badly do you think the business is struggling?"

Bob frowned. "It's hard to say. The new windows can't be cheap. I wondered if there was more to the story the first night we were here. Aunt Lydia is very frugal and has been especially that way since Uncle Harvey got sick. Getting new windows is nice, but not a necessity, you know? I thought I saw some bits of broken glass when we were outside the window after we first arrived. That's why I was on the floor. I was checking to see if there was any glass inside too." He sighed. "Enough shop-talk. Let's enjoy our walk."

Cari nodded and decided to change the subject. "I can't get over how beautiful it is here. It's not like I want to move here, but I would never get tired of looking at that lake."

Bob smiled. "It is pretty great. Ready to get some dinner?"

"I'm pretty hungry. We worked hard out on the lake today."

Chapter 7

C ari woke up to the sunlight streaming into the room from a gap in the curtains. She felt her stomach rumble and was surprised. She tried the whitefish at Mel's last night and the lemon caper sauce had been amazing. While she didn't normally eat dessert, she couldn't pass up the slice of decadent chocolate cake she had seen the waiter bring to another table.

Not surprisingly, Bob was already in the shower. She knew he rarely slept past eight and was excited to go out in the kayak again. Her arms felt less excited, but she was looking forward to seeing Specter Island. She pushed the covers back and swung her feet over the bed just as Bob emerged from the bathroom.

"Good morning. Ready to get back on the lake?" Bob asked.

She flexed her sore muscles. "I am. Let me grab a shower and we can get some breakfast."

Cari picked out some clothes for the day and walked past Bob into the bathroom. She almost laughed out loud when she saw her hair. Her curls were frizzed out in multiple directions. It looked like she had tried to tease it out big like they used to in the seventies. *This could take a hot minute to get under control.*

She turned on the water and brushed her teeth while she waited for it to warm up. Her freshman year roommate had teased her about brushing her teeth first thing before eating breakfast. Cari smiled. Her grandmother had always done that and she had adopted the habit after spending a week with her one summer as a child.

She stuck her hand into the shower to confirm the water was warm, then stepped inside. Her detangling shampoo worked wonders to calm down her frizzy curls, though her arms didn't appreciate the extra movement. Once out of the shower, she decided to anticipate the wind on the lake and wove her hair into a French braid. Her stomach growled again, so she quickly threw on her clothes and exited the bathroom.

"That was faster than I expected after seeing your hair when you woke up," Bob laughed.

"It was quite a sight. Ready for breakfast? I just need to get on my socks and shoes."

"I'm going to go down and pick up our picnic. I'll meet you outside of the restaurant."

"Sounds good. See you down there."

Cari pulled on her socks and shoes. Her phone was plugged in on the nightstand. She picked it up and removed the charger. The screen showed she had a missed call from Genevieve, but no voicemail. She unlocked the screen and saw her friend had texted.

Your photos are amazing! I clearly need to add Wisconsin to my bucket list. This training program is intense. Loving every minute. Talk soon.

Cari smiled. She knew Genevieve would make a great FBI agent and hoped the people in charge of the training program recognized her skills and assets. She gave her friend's text a thumbs up and slipped her phone into her pocket.

Bob was sitting on a chair outside of the restaurant with his backpack when she got downstairs. She smiled as she walked over to join him. Her stomach rumbled audibly as soon as she reached his chair.

"I'll take that as a hint," he laughed.

She grinned. "I can't believe I'm hungry again after stuffing myself last night, but here we are."

They took a seat at one of the window tables. The waiter from the previous morning arrived almost immediately with two glasses of water and a carafe of coffee. Cari smiled at her.

"Good morning, Becky! I will definitely take a cup of coffee," Cari greeted her.

Becky placed the two water glasses in front of them and then flipped over the coffee cups. "Do you want to order from the menu today?"

Bob nodded. "Yes, please. We're ready for a big breakfast this morning."

Becky smiled and then turned to Cari. "I'll grab two menus and bring your coffee additions with them."

"She's really nice," Cari said after she walked away. "Remind me, what is our kayaking plan today?"

"We're going to head straight for the cave where you saw the drawings, look around as much as you'd like, then get over to Specter Island for a picnic."

Becky dropped off two menus and some honey and milk for Cari's coffee.

"Thank you," Bob told her.

"I'll be back in a few minutes to take your order. I heard you were going kayaking again today, so I'll make sure the kitchen knows to get your breakfast out fast."

"Thanks, Becky," Cari responded.

She opened her menu. The restaurant had a plethora of options for breakfast. She wished she could try all of them, but eggs, bacon, and toast seemed like a good choice to keep energized for another day of kayaking.

"I'm hoping to get some more photos of the drawings today. I wonder how old they are. I'm kind of surprised they're still around given the amount of water that rushes into the caves regularly."

"Whatever paint they used was probably more of a dye. I bet it stained the rocks."

"That makes sense."

Becky returned to their table. "Ready to order?"

Cari spoke up first. "I'll get the Boarding House Big Breakfast with bacon and wheat toast."

"Make that two," Bob said holding up two fingers.

"Coming right up."

* * * * *

Lydia drummed her fingers on her desk. She looked at the list she'd made about talking to Jack. She should have called him weeks ago when the first break-in happened. He could have advised her on security companies and helped her stay calm through the process. She felt even more foolish for trying to manage everything herself. She balled her hands into fists and clenched them, hoping to steel her nerves. She couldn't put this off any longer. She picked up the phone and dialed his number by memory.

"Lydia? Is everything okay? You rarely call on a weekday," her brother's deep voice boomed into the phone.

"Hi, Jack. Sorry to just call out of the blue. Um, no. Everything is not really okay." She sighed before continuing. "I should have called sooner—"

"Oh, no…is it Bob? I just remembered he's out there with his girlfriend. Did something happen? Did the proposal flop? Did—"

"No, no. It's nothing about Bob. I need some help, Jack. With The Boarding House…" she trailed off.

"Of course, Lydia. What do you need? We can come out there; Margie would love to visit too."

"You don't need to rush out here. You have your own lives. I just…I need some advice."

She took a deep breath and told him everything: the break-ins, the property taxes, the loss of business. To his credit, he listened without interrupting or questioning at any point. She let out a big sigh when she finished.

"I need to find a security company and get cameras installed. I started looking into it yesterday and requested quotes online from a couple places. Those are probably in my inbox. Bob tried to help me look at them yesterday—"

"Bob knows all about this?"

"Yes, he's been a dear. Cari too. She helped get the sheriff's department involved. I'm hoping to hear from them soon too."

"My goodness, Lyd. You should have called sooner. I know this is your business and it's your call how you run it, but you don't have to do it all alone. I love The Boarding House too. And we're family. Let me talk to Margie. We can grab a quick flight to Minneapolis easily. I'll text you our travel details…uh, do you have room for us there?"

"Of course I have room for you."

"Have you talked to your kids about this?"

"Paul is in Europe; there's no reason to bother him with this right now. And Ellie is not concerned with the business. She's living her best life as a dancer in Toronto."

"Okay, I get it. I'll be in touch."

"Thank you, Jack. Give Margie my best."

She ended the call and laid back in her chair. She had been dreading telling Jack about her missteps, but it was a relief to no longer be navigating the crisis alone. She checked her email and found the quotes from the two security companies. They both offered multiple options depending on how many cameras and the level of support she wanted. She decided to hold off on reviewing them until Jack arrived.

* * * * *

Cari and Bob had gotten into the water much quicker today than yesterday. Even though her arms were sore, she felt more familiar with paddling across the lake and felt like they were traveling faster too. The kayak they rented today only had the storage space or bulkhead in the front. She told Bob she would be very careful with his backpack and not let any harm come to it, but she still wanted to sit in the front seat. After his reluctance with Dale the day before, she expected him to object, but he passed it right over to her. Unfortunately, Bob was still uptight about something. He had been almost silent on the drive over to meet Dale and get the kayak. Her thoughts drifted back to Lydia's mention of someone named Contessa. It sounded like maybe they'd been more than friends. She tried to push aside the jealous thoughts running through her head.

"It's such a beautiful day. I'm so excited to see Specter Island," she called back to Bob from the front of the kayak.

Bob mumbled a response.

"What?"

"I said I was excited too," he told her.

"Did you think of a reason why someone would dig inside the cave?"

"No."

Cari tried to stay positive. She felt like she was annoying him and couldn't figure out why. "I hope I can get better photos than I did yesterday. I was so hungry; I think my hands were a little shaky."

She heard Bob groan. "Yesterday was a complete disaster."

"No! I had a great time. I wasn't trying to be critical."

Bob didn't respond. Cari bit her lip. Maybe it would be better not to make conversation. She was having to shout anyway, which probably made her comment seem less light-hearted. She looked along the shoreline and thought she recognized the bend where they saw the second cave from the day before.

"Is this the right place to turn for the cave?"

"This is it," Bob replied flatly. "Let's paddle on the right and make a left turn."

"Aye, aye, Captain!" Cari called out.

Just as she plunged her paddle into the water, she heard a loud noise. It almost sounded like a helicopter, but that didn't seem right. She looked up. The cloudless sky was free of aircraft. She started to turn to look over her shoulder when Bob cried out.

"Cari! Look out! Lean—"

In that instant, a speedboat roared past them. Its wake sent a wave that crashed into the kayak, making it lurch forward and to the left, almost tipping over. Cari felt herself being forced forward with the momentum and her head slammed into the front of the kayak. She felt dizzy and her vision clouded. Bob was calling out to her about something. She tried to put her paddle in the water, but she felt exhausted. She felt her eyelids start to droop and the world went black.

* * * * *

Bob watched in horror as Cari's head slammed into the kayak. He tried to ask her if she was okay, but her head was dropping as though she was falling asleep. *She's about to pass out*. His anger flared at the driver of the speedboat. He had broken every rule of etiquette Bob knew by driving so fast and so close to their kayak.

He looked around to see if Dale or Rich were nearby, but knew it was probably a long shot. They had a tour group of twelve people they were taking around the lake today. Bob had assured them they would be fine on their own. He regretted that now.

"Cari? Are you awake? Cari!"

Her head was still slumped forward along with her shoulders. He could see her shoulders rise and fall, so he knew she was still breathing. Bob didn't know if she was bleeding and couldn't reach her from the back. Her paddle had slipped from her hands, but thankfully, was still balanced across her lap in the kayak. He needed to turn the kayak around and get Cari some help. He ran a hand over his face trying to calm down and think rationally. It had taken them over ninety minutes to get this far with both of them paddling. He was stronger than Cari, but one paddle was still less powerful than two. If she was bleeding, she needed attention sooner than he could get to shore. The shoreline on this part of the lake was all rocks. He wouldn't be able to get the kayak ashore and get to his phone until they reached the sandy beach where they had put into the water. He didn't think she had a serious neck injury, but it was best to be cautious just in case. Paddling across the lake could result in a more serious injury if she had hurt her neck or spine. Cari had put her phone in the zippered pocket of her life vest so she could have it to take photos, but he had kept his in the backpack and then let her store it in the front bulkhead. He had noticed his behavior with the backpack yesterday had made Cari suspicious, so he put the little ring box in his pocket and opted to keep his phone in the backpack. He rationalized that she could get to her phone, so it was fine. Now he regretted choosing the ring over his phone. He just needed to make one phone call.

Siri! Bob realized he could possibly talk to Siri through Cari's Apple watch. It was supposed to respond to her voice, but maybe he could get it to work with the right words. He had to try.

"Hey, Siri. Emergency. Call 911."

Bob strained to listen over the sound of the wind. Maybe he wasn't loud enough.

"Hey, Siri! Emergency! Call 911!" he shouted towards Cari's wrist.

He heard a faint ringing sound and almost cried with relief. He hoped the emergency operator wouldn't put him on hold. He knew they were often fielding multiple calls at once, but this part of Wisconsin was pretty remote…

"911, what is your emergency? Hello?"

"Hello! This is Bob Hursley. I'm calling from, um, part way out onto Lake Superior. My girlfriend hit her head when a speedboat—"

"I'm sorry. I can barely hear you. Can you speak up?"

"Please. I'm trying to yell toward my girlfriend's Apple watch. She is unconscious. She hit her head."

"Okay, I understand. My name is Natalie. I'm going to help you. Is she bleeding?"

"I don't know. She's in the front of the kayak. I'm in the back. It will probably take me close to two hours to get her back to our car."

"I'm tracking your location. Is there someone else you can call to get to you more quickly? We don't really have a water rescue team here."

"Um, well, I can't really call anyone. I can't reach her watch. I asked Siri to make an emergency call." Bob's voice felt strained from continuously shouting. "But maybe you could call the owner of the kayak company for me? She's out on the water right now. You could direct her to us."

"Give me the number, Mr. Hursley."

Bob flipped his paddle over and found the phone number. "Okay, here it is." He shouted the digits out two at a time and waited for her to repeat them back.

"Okay, I'm going to set up a three-way call, Mr. Hursley. Just give me one second. Let's hope your kayak gal answers."

Bob said a prayer under his breath and waited. He mentally begged Cari to wake up. How long had it been since the speedboat passed them?

"This is Dale. What's up?"

"Hello, Dale. This is Natalie with emergency services. One of your customers is in some trouble and needs your help getting ashore. Mr. Hursley, can you direct Dale to your location?"

92

"Dale! It is great to hear your voice. We're out past the fifth bend, near the second cave that's big enough to fit a kayak."

"Dude, what happened? You said you'd be fine out here on your own."

"I'm sorry," Bob shouted. "We got passed by a speedboat."

"A speedboat? I saw that guy go by. I didn't realize…sorry. How can I help?"

Natalie spoke up. "Dale, if you could reach Mr. Hursley and his girlfriend, that's really what we need. We need to assess her injuries."

"You got it. I'll let Rich take over my tour and be on my way in a jiffy."

"I think she hung up, Bob. Do you know if she has a motorized boat?"

"I'm not sure. I hope so."

"I'll stay on the line with you until she arrives."

"Thanks. I'm going to save my voice. I'll shout if I need anything."

"Roger that."

Bob looked up at Cari. *C'mon, Cari. Wake up!* He patted his life vest wishing he had something that could help her, but he knew the pockets were empty.

"Cari? Can you hear me? You hit your head. Please wake up. I need to know that you're okay. It's time to wake up, Cari…"

Chapter 8

Cari's legs felt so heavy, like she was running through mud or molasses or maybe quicksand. She was trying to get up the hills near The Boarding House again, but she was moving so slowly. She heard someone's voice and saw Bob had pulled even with her. Normally, she was the one trying to encourage him to keep up the pace. Now he was passing her?

"C'mon, Cari. You can do it. Get up."

"I'm trying, Bob. I'm feeling slow today. Like my legs are made of lead."

"C'mon, Cari. Please. Wake up. Wake up. Wake—"

Cari's eyes flicked open. She felt her legs moving irregularly in her seat. Where was she?

"Cari! Oh my God, Cari. Are you okay?" Bob's voice was full of emotion.

"Cari, can you hear me?" Another voice spoke from the kayak.

"Um, who was that?" Cari turned her head.

"Is your neck okay? Don't move." Bob cautioned.

"It's fine. I can feel my toes, my fingers, my legs...my head. Ouch. What happened?"

Cari put a hand up to her head and felt something tacky. She pulled her hand down and saw blood on her fingertips.

"I'm bleeding."

"I was afraid of that. You hit your head pretty hard when the speedboat went past us. You might have a concussion." Bob told her.

"Cari? This is Natalie with emergency services. I realize you're probably in a state of shock, but can you answer some questions for me?"

"I can try."

"You said you can feel all your extremities, correct?"

"Yes."

"That's great. Now, very slowly, I want you to turn your body and look at Mr. Hursley behind you."

"Okay."

Cari slowly rotated herself at the waist and turned to look at Bob. He was wiping tears from his eyes and his face paled when she faced him.

"Oh, Cari. That's a pretty bad cut on your forehead. Dale is on her way out here." Bob turned his head to listen. "That might be her boat now."

"Okay, Cari. Rotate back forward while Mr. Hursley keeps an eye out for Ms. Dale."

Cari giggled. She didn't see Dale as someone who wanted to be addressed as a Ms. She was rough and tumble, ready for an adventure. "Ms. Dale" sounded like an old school marm.

"Is everything okay?"

"Yes, sorry. What's next?"

"I want you to put your index finger out in front of your face and move it slowly to the right until you can't see it anymore."

Cari did as Natalie requested. Her arm was fully extended to her right side when she lost sight of her finger.

"I made it all the way to the right. Want me to repeat it on the left?"

"Yes, please."

Cari repeated the process with her left hand and was happy to report that she hadn't lost any of her peripheral vision on that side either.

"Dale is here, Natalie. She'll get us back to shore," Bob reported from the back of the kayak.

"Do you need me to send an ambulance to meet you?" Natalie asked.

"No!" Cari responded before Bob. "If I need medical attention, we'll drive ourselves. I think I'm fine. Really."

Bob hesitated before responding. "Okay, Natalie. We'll call you back if something changes. Thank you so much for your help."

"My pleasure, Mr. Hursley. Take care, Cari."

The call ended. Cari let out a sigh. She was starting to feel a bit tired again and figured Bob's diagnosis of a concussion was probably correct.

"All right, friends. Let's get your kayak tied off to my boat and get you on board."

Bob grabbed a rope from Dale and looped it around the bar in the middle of the kayak. He handed it back. Dale used another tool to grip the side of their kayak in two places to keep it steady.

"Okay, first, hand me your oars. Then, unzip your skirts."

Cari bit her lip to keep from laughing as she undid the zipper on the black kayak skirt.

"Now, Cari, let's get you over here first. I want you to very slowly push yourself up to standing. Then, grab my hand and step over to my vessel."

Cari did as she instructed, but as she stood, she felt light-headed. Dale grabbed her hand as she started listing to the side.

"Easy there. Pretty nasty bump on your head. Here we go. Up and over." She held her hand in a firm grip and put her left hand under her arm to keep her steady. Cari placed her left foot into the boat and then stepped over with her right too. She had noticed the woman's strong arms when they first met and was thankful the middle-aged woman was in such great shape.

"There you go. All right, Bob. Your turn now…don't worry about your backpack. It's still safe inside the bulkhead. We'll get it out when we get to shore."

Bob grabbed Dale's hand and pulled himself up into the boat too. Dale double-checked the kayak was still secured to her boat. Then she sat back down behind the wheel.

"Okay, let's get back to shore. I'm sorry your picnic got spoiled." Dale said to them.

Cari blinked in the sunlight and felt on top of her head for her sunglasses. Frowning she leaned towards the kayak to see if they might have fallen into where she'd been sitting. She could only see the black skirt.

Bob crossed the boat and sat next to her. "Is everything okay? Dale, do you have any bottles of water?"

Dale jerked her head towards a cooler behind the seat next to hers. Bob got up and pulled out two bottles. He opened one and handed it to Cari. She took a drink and then put the lid back on.

"I'm okay. I just…I think I lost my sunglasses when I hit my head. The sun is really bright and squinting makes my head hurt more." Her shoulders sagged. "I'm sorry for being such a wimp."

"No! You're not a wimp. This is not your fault. The driver of that boat! He was reckless. He should never have been so close to our kayak at that speed."

"Did you get a good look at his boat? I saw a speedboat pass by earlier, but who knows if it's the same guy?" Dale remarked.

Bob grimaced. "I hate to say this, but I didn't. One minute we were turning left, and the next we almost capsized. The boat might have had a blue stripe on it, but the water is blue. I could just be remembering that."

"We still need to report it. The Coast Guard might have seen him if he was going as fast as it sounds."

"The Coast Guard operates on the Lakes?" Cari asked groggily.

"Oh yeah. The Ninth District is in charge of all the Great Lakes, the St. Lawrence River, the water boundary between us and Canada…it's a big assignment. I mean, it's not an ocean, but it's still a lot of area." Dale told her.

"Learn something every day," Cari giggled, then winced. "Ouch. Whoever said 'laughter is the best medicine' never had a head injury."

"We'll be back at the shore in just a few minutes. I'll unhook your kayak and we can get it dragged back in. Once you have everything out of the bulkhead, you can get on your way to the hospital. I can give your information to the Coast Guard. They'll probably want to interview you."

* * * * *

Lydia let her cell phone drop onto her desk and sank into her office chair. She squeezed her trembling hands together. Bob's voice echoed through her mind. *"…been in an accident. The kayak nearly capsized…concussion…hospital…"* When her nephew called a couple months ago to request a room at the bed and breakfast, she thought it was the perfect romantic getaway for a proposal. Now, she wished she had told him to go to Hawaii instead.

She picked up her phone and checked it again to see if Jack and Margie had landed yet. She hoped they hadn't spent too much on the last-minute tickets, but Margie claimed to have used some of their travel points on the tickets. They would still have a four-hour drive from the airport. She put the phone back down and drummed her fingers on the desk. Bob had said Cari needed to be evaluated for a concussion, but he was pretty certain she had one. She also might need stitches on her forehead from where her face struck the

98

kayak. Lydia's eyes filled with tears. The poor thing. Maybe it wouldn't scar. Her desk phone rang and startled her back to reality.

"The Boarding House. This is Lydia. How can I help you today?"

"Ms. Fairchild. It's Deputy Yarrow with the Lake County Sheriff's Department. We got a match for one of the prints we pulled. Do you think you could come by and look at a photo array?"

"Right now?"

"The sooner the better. We'd also like your guest to take a look at it. The one who startled him yesterday."

Lydia's shoulders sagged. "Do you have a name?"

"I'd rather not give you a name over the phone. It's not that I don't trust you, but it's tempting to look someone up once you hear their name and that could bias your viewing later. Is your guest still in town?"

Lydia bit her lip. "Oh, oh dear. I don't…"

"Did she already check out?"

"No, but she was in an accident this morning. She hit her head and may have a concussion."

"How awful! A car accident?" Yarrow asked her.

"No, it was while they were kayaking. A motorboat zipped by them too closely. The wake made the kayak nearly tip over and she hit her head on the nose of it."

"Dang! That sounds terrifying. I'll tell you what. Let me get this photo array together and I'll see if we can swing by with it tomorrow…if she feels up to it."

"That sounds great. Should I call you in the morning?"

"I'll give you a ring after we get the ball rolling tomorrow. I have a few other things to take care of each morning."

"Okay, I look forward to hearing from you again. Thank you, Deputy Yarrow."

"My pleasure, ma'am."

The call ended. Lydia felt partly relieved they had a suspect, but she remembered Cari saying she hadn't seen the man's face. She wasn't sure what good it would do if no one could identify him as being in the room during the burglary.

* * * * *

Cari watched Bob pacing alongside the examination table. She could hear him muttering under his breath. The nearest hospital was in Duluth, but she had spotted an urgent care center before they reached it. The nurse had taken Cari's vitals and listened to their summary of the incident. She typed it into a laptop and said the doctor would be in shortly. Cari wasn't expecting "shortly" to be soon. She closed her eyes again. Not because she was tired but because the lights in the room made her head hurt more.

"Are you okay?" Bob asked as he rushed to her side.

She slowly opened her eyes. "I'm fine, Bob. My eyes are sensitive to the lights in here, so I closed them. I didn't faint. I promise."

"Of course, I'm sorry. I hope the doctor gets in here soon. I can't believe that guy."

"The doctor?" Cari asked with confusion.

"No, the driver of the speedboat. I wonder if they found him yet."

"They might never identify him. It's okay. I'll still go kayaking with you again." She smiled at him with her eyes closed.

Bob muttered something under his breath and gave her a light kiss. She wished he could calm down. This trip had been nothing but stressful for him so far. She felt like she was a magnet for trouble. First the break-in, now a kayaking accident!

A quick knock sounded at the door and someone entered before Cari could respond. She forced her eyes open again and saw a young woman with straight dark hair and tan skin. Cari tried to read the name on her badge, but it made her head hurt, so she waited for her to introduce herself.

"Ms. Turnlyle?" Cari nodded and winced in pain. "Ouch, looks like you hit your head pretty hard today. The nurse has listed light-sensitivity, a headache, loss of consciousness, and some disorientation following the collision. Anything else?"

"No. That about covers it," Cari told her.

"Forgive me. I'm Dr. Isana. It sounds like you have a concussion. Let's get a look at your pupils. I'm sorry about the light. I'll do it as quickly as I can."

Cari looked forward as Dr. Isana shined a pen light in her eyes. It felt like someone pushed a pin into her brain. She felt tears filling her eyes and willed herself not to cry.

"Your pupils are still a bit dilated. I'm going to do a quick x-ray to make sure you don't have a skull fracture—"

Bob coughed and cleared his throat from the chair next to the table. The doctor swung her head to look at him quizzically.

"Everything okay?"

"Yes, sorry," Bob mumbled.

"And you are?"

"I'm Bob Hursley…her, uh, boyfriend."

"Nice to meet you, Mr. Hursley. Why don't you wait here while we go do this x-ray? Ms. Turnlyle, are you okay on your feet?"

"Yes, ma'am."

Cari scooted to the edge of the table and stood up. She'd never had an x-ray before. She wondered if the doctor would let her do it with her eyes closed.

* * * * *

Lydia scanned the street outside for a sign of Bob's rental vehicle. He had texted almost forty-five minutes ago to say they were on their way from the urgent care center near Duluth. It was rush hour, so maybe traffic was slowing them down. She busied herself by straightening the items on the display shelf outside her office. The cleaning staff usually dusted the shelving once a week, but she could see dust had settled around the items. She walked down the hallway to the supply closet and found a rag and dusting spray. It couldn't hurt to give things a once-over while she waited.

As she wiped the dust off the Christmas ornaments, notebooks, and shelving, she glanced over at her office. The manila envelope from the realtor glared back at her from her desk. Her hand tightened around the spray bottle causing it to spray onto a stack of postcards.

"Darn it!" she hissed, quickly wiping the oil off the stack.

The top postcard had already started to curl on the sides. She picked it up and stuck it in her apron pocket. She needed to relax. She wasn't going to lose the business. Shaking her head in frustration, she grabbed the rag and shoved it into her other pocket. She walked back to the supply closet and returned the spray bottle, then tossed the rag into the pile of laundry in the utility room. The front door to The Boarding House opened just as she reached the lobby. Bob held the door for Cari while keeping one hand under her elbow. She was wearing ill-fitting sunglasses, but Lydia could see a bandage above her left eye.

"Oh! I'm so glad you're back safely," she rushed over to Bob and squeezed his free hand. "How are you, Cari? Can I get you anything?"

Cari gave her a small smile. "I got these sweet shades from the nurse at the urgent care. But, seriously, I'm okay, Lydia. I've been better, but right now, I'd just like to go rest in our room."

"Of course. If you need anything, just have Bob give me a ring. I'm so sorry to hear about your accident."

"Actually, now that I think about it, would it be okay to have dinner in our room tonight? I just don't feel like being around people or getting dressed up."

Lydia saw Bob's shoulders slump a bit out of the corner of her eye. He had asked for a special table tonight so that he could propose. She knew he must be disappointed.

"Of course, dear. Bob, figure out your orders and bring them down to me. I'll have the kitchen get it together for you."

"Thank you, Aunt Lydia. I'm going to help Cari up to our room, then I'll come back down with the order," he said quietly.

Lydia watched them climb the stairs to the top floor. She put her hands on her hips and tried to decide what to do next. Before she could make up her mind, her cell phone buzzed with an incoming call. *Jack. Finally.*

"Jack! I've been wondering where you are. I thought your flight was supposed to land at three?"

"I wish. Lyd, it was just one thing after another. First, we had a small delay because they were holding our flight for some passengers whose connection was delayed. Then, we had to wait for their bags. We finally pulled away from the gate and got in line to take off—that's when I texted you before. But then we circled back around to the gate. Someone on our plane brought their own alcohol on board and was doing some imbibing."

"You're kidding!" Lydia laughed.

"No. I mean, they always make that announcement, but I've never been on a flight where someone actually tested the policy. Ten out of ten, would not recommend it. They had to be removed from the flight. I should have texted you then, but they made it sound like it would just be a minute or two. It was another hour. Sorry for being a poor communicator."

"Sounds like quite the adventure. So, where are you now?"

"We are in the rental car. I've got my phone hooked up to the Bluetooth and Margie is my navigator."

Margie's muffled voice came over the line. "Hi, Lydia! Can't wait to see you."

"Hello, Margie. Likewise. I guess we'll see you at nine or so?" she asked them.

"The GPS says 9:12 right now. I'm going to try to beat it, though." She could hear the competitiveness in his voice.

"Well, drive safe. We're not...going anywhere." Lydia hesitated.

"Is everything okay, Lyd?" Margie asked with concern.

Lydia didn't want to shock them over the phone, but she didn't want to keep the accident from them either. She bit her lip. Just as she was about to respond, Bob got back downstairs.

"Oh, Bob just got here. Let me check in with him. We'll see you soon." She ended the call.

Bob handed her a slip of paper with their order on it. "Cari isn't very hungry, which is pretty normal for someone with a concussion. It can give you some nausea. She had a banana from our picnic lunch earlier, but nothing else."

"Did she end up needing stitches?" Lydia asked him.

"They debated about it but ultimately decided to give her three stitches. The doctor said it was her best chance at avoiding a scar in the long term," he paused. "Who was on the phone? Sorry, that's not any of my business."

"No! No, it's fine. That was your parents. I called your father this morning. He and Margie flew out here and are on their way from Minneapolis now."

Bob's face brightened a bit. "Oh, wow! I'm glad you decided to call Dad. I wasn't expecting to see them while we were here. Uh, I should probably let Cari know they're coming instead of letting them surprise her."

"Don't wake her just for that. I'll get your order over to the kitchen. One of the servers will bring it up in an hour or so, okay?"

"Thanks, Aunt Lydia. I'm sorry we're adding to your woes."

"Not at all. I'm glad you're both okay."

Remembering Deputy Yarrow's call from earlier, she placed a hand on Bob's arm before he walked away.

"Was there something else?" Bob looked at her with concern.

"I almost forgot. Deputy Yarrow called to say they got a match from one of the prints. He wouldn't give me a name in case I was tempted to look the person up. He was hoping Cari might feel up for looking at a…what did he call it…" she pursed her lips trying to remember.

"A lineup? A photo array?" Bob asked.

"Photo array! That was it. He said he could bring it by tomorrow. What do you think? He's going to call me in the morning to check in."

"I'll mention it to Cari. I'm sure she'll want to help. I'm going to go check on her now. Thanks, Aunt Lydia."

* * * * *

Bob quietly opened the door to their room. He crossed over to the sitting area and took a seat on the sofa. Cari was fast asleep on the bed. He could already see the bruises forming around her eyes from the collision. He'd never thought of Cari as vain, but he knew she would be disappointed to see how her face looked the next morning. The white steri-strips above her left eye stood out in stark contrast to the bruising and swelling of the rest of her face.

His suitcase was open on the luggage stand next to the sofa. He looked at Cari again to be sure she was asleep, then unzipped the small interior pocket inside his suitcase. His fingers closed around the small, black box. Double-checking on Cari, he slowly pulled the ring box from its hiding place and opened it. The triple-diamond setting ring sparkled at him from the box. He had practiced proposing to Cari in his head umpteen times in the last month. He wanted the proposal to be romantic and memorable,

105

but everything he'd planned so far had been a disaster. He snapped the box closed when he heard a groan from the bed.

His eyes flicked to Cari while he deftly slipped the ring box back into the little pocket. He slowly exhaled when he realized she wasn't awake. She must have groaned in her sleep. He continued to watch her while he pulled his cell phone from his pocket. His parents hadn't texted about coming out to Wisconsin, even though they knew he was here with Cari. Maybe they didn't want to interrupt their vacation. He put his cell phone away and looked at his watch. He had time to take a quick shower before their dinner arrived. Maybe he could wash some of his anxiety away in the process too. He grabbed a change of clothes from his suitcase and walked quietly to the bathroom. Luckily the shower was in a second room beyond the first door to the bathroom. It would help to further muffle the sound and hopefully not disturb Cari.

He turned on the shower and then stripped off his clothes. The water heated up quickly and it felt good to wash the lake water off. It had been a long day and nothing was going as he'd imagined it. He let the water run over him for a few minutes while he mulled over ideas of how to salvage the rest of their trip. The ferry ride to Specter Island was still two days away. He hoped Cari would feel up for it by then. He had booked that excursion as soon as he confirmed the reservation at The Boarding House with Aunt Lydia. The ferry to Specter Island was one of the more popular tourist attractions and wouldn't have any other openings during their time here. He didn't think Cari would be able to kayak out to it any more.

After finishing his shower, he toweled off and slipped into his change of clothes. He quickly combed his hair and noticed it was almost time to get it cut again. He had never liked his naturally curly hair and kept it short to keep people from seeing any curls. He set the comb down and tried to open the door softly, but when he stepped back into the room, he saw Cari was already awake.

"I'm sorry for waking you up. I tried to be quiet."

She gave him a faint smile. "I literally just woke up and it wasn't because of the shower."

"How are you feeling?" he asked as he gently sat on the bed and took her hand.

"I'm actually pretty hungry, which is a relief. The nausea from before was terrible."

Bob grinned. "I'm really glad to hear that. How does your head feel?"

"I want to say worse than it looks, but it probably looks pretty bad. It still hurts." She gave a little shrug. "When is dinner coming up?"

He checked his watch. "Should be any moment now. Would you like me to go check?"

"No, that's okay. Just sit with me. Do you think we can use the coffee table?"

"Works for me."

A light knock sounded on the door and Bob got up to answer it. Lydia stood outside with a tray of food. A waitress was behind her with two glasses of water. Bob swung the door open wider and gestured towards the coffee table.

"We thought we could eat on the coffee table. Thank you for bringing our meal upstairs."

"You are most welcome. We'll just get these plates and glasses set down and be out of your hair." Lydia told him.

"It smells delicious. Thank you so much." Cari said as she got up from the bed.

Bob waited for his aunt and the waitress to leave before sitting down across from Cari at the coffee table. She was already unrolling her silverware.

"I'm famished. I'm glad I let you talk me into ordering a full meal and not just a salad. What a day!"

"It has been a pretty crazy trip so far. I thought it would be a great place to relax, but it seems like we've just bounced from one problem to the next."

"I'm having a wonderful time," she said between bites. "Now, eat your dinner."

Bob picked up his mushroom and Swiss cheese hamburger and took a bite. It was just as he'd remembered it from childhood. He swallowed and paused before taking another bite.

"By the way, Aunt Lydia mentioned the sheriff's office called about the prints they pulled yesterday."

"Yeah?" Cari asked with her mouth full.

"They got a hit on one. They wouldn't tell Aunt Lydia the name to keep from biasing her viewing. They're hoping you'll feel up for looking at a photo array."

Cari slowly lowered her fork. "Tonight?"

"No, not tonight. Tomorrow morning. They said they could bring it to you."

"I'm happy to look at it, but I didn't see his face ever. You are more likely to have seen him on the street."

Bob nodded in agreement. "True, but I wasn't paying much attention to people. They'll probably show it to all of us. We'll see what happens."

They continued eating in silence. Bob chewed slowly and prayed the next day would be free of disasters.

108

Chapter 9

Cari woke up and winced in pain. It took her a moment to remember the prior day's events. The urgent care doctor recommended acetaminophen or ibuprofen for pain. Thankfully, she always traveled with a bottle of ibuprofen. She pushed the covers back and eased herself out of bed. She was relieved when the room didn't spin like it had the night before.

She slipped into the bathroom and pulled the door closed behind her. Bob was still sleeping and she didn't want to wake him. She flicked on the light and instantly regretted it. Her eyes were still feeling some light sensitivity and squinting did not help. Taking a deep breath, she relaxed her eyelids and slowly opened them again. Her hand flew to her mouth when she saw her reflection in the mirror. Dark purple bruises encircled both eyes and her nose even looked swollen, but maybe she was imagining that. The cut above her eye was a bit inflamed as well, but it was virtually nothing compared to her raccoon eyes. She pinched her lips together, trying not to cry, but the longer she stared at her reflection, the harder it was. Her eyes filled with tears and she gave up stopping them. A hand squeezed her shoulder, causing her to jump.

"Sorry, I didn't mean to startle you," Bob said gently.

Cari tried to wipe the tears off her face with her hands. "I'm fine. I just, uh, I…"

Bob put his arms around her and she let her right cheek settle onto his chest. She felt foolish for crying about how she looked. She knew the bruising would subside in a few days, but for now, it was a reminder of yesterday's events. After half a minute, she pulled back and choked out a laugh.

"Lucky for you, I haven't put on any makeup yet. I left a little puddle on your shirt."

Bob kissed her gently on her lips and hugged her one more time. "It's okay to be upset about it. Yesterday was scary for me too."

"I wasn't really scared in the moment, though. I mean, I *was* unconscious for part of it, but then I was just focused on getting to shore, seeing a doctor, getting back here...sleeping." She sighed. "It was a long day...looks like I'll be taking a hiatus from all of the selfies for a few days."

"How about I go see if we can get breakfast brought up here? Unless you feel like eating downstairs?"

"Breakfast in the room sounds perfect. I'm going to shower first."

"What do you want to order?"

"Those scones were amazing, but if you see something else that looks good, go for it."

He laughed. "Scones it is."

Bob closed the door. She turned on the bathroom fan and then reached into the shower to start the water. She'd been so tired the night before, she had put on her pajamas and crawled into bed after eating dinner. Her hand absentmindedly went to where her locket usually sat on her chest. When her fingers didn't feel it, she felt a brief moment of panic thinking she had lost it in the lake the day before. Then she remembered taking it off after brushing her teeth. She looked down at the countertop and saw it coiled in the little box that held the extra soap bottles. She needed to give

Grandmother a call today. She felt bad for not telling her about the accident yesterday, but she was too tired to talk on the phone then.

Sighing, she tossed her clothing aside and stepped into the shower. She hoped the water wouldn't make the cut on her forehead sting, but it would be worth it not to feel so grubby. She stepped under the water and tried to relax as it ran down her body. She didn't want to stay in too long. She knew Bob would be back with breakfast soon.

As she lathered up her hair, Cari tried to remember what she saw before the wake of the speedboat made her hit her head. She closed her eyes and reimagined the scene. *We'd just made the left turn toward the cave. I was saying something to Bob, or was he talking to me? And then he shouted and then...I woke up with a gash on my head.*

"Ugh!" Cari balled up her fists and groaned.

She hadn't seen anything. The boat had been behind her and then she was unconscious. She finished showering and turned off the water. The bathroom was full of steam, which was pleasant as it kept her from seeing her face in the mirror. She wrapped the towel around herself and grabbed her locket off the counter. She fastened it around her neck and padded out to the room to get some clean clothes.

After getting dressed, she unplugged her phone and pulled up her grandmother's number. She tried to work out the words she wanted to say before hitting the call button, but she just kept getting emotional. She decided to just wing it.

"Cari! What have you been up to? We didn't get any photos yesterday and figured you must be having too much fun out in Wisconsin. How are you, my dear?"

Cari swallowed and willed herself to relax. "Hi, Grandmother. It's great to hear your voice—"

"What's wrong? You sound upset."

Cari lifted her chin and tried again to stay calm. "I'm fine, it's just, well…" she sighed. "We went kayaking again yesterday and had a little accident. Don't worry! Obviously, I'm fine. I'm sorry I didn't call you yesterday. I have a concussion and was pretty tired after going to urgent care and talking to the Coast Guard on the phone…let's see…getting stitches."

"Stitches! Oh dear. I thought you were on the lake…I don't understand. How did you hit your head?"

"We got passed by a speedboat and the wake made me ram my head into the kayak. It was kind of a freak accident, but I'm fine now. Really. How are you?"

"Well, my heart is racing a bit after hearing that story. I don't know what I'm going to do with you girls."

"Bob is taking great care of me, Grandmother." Cari glanced at the door when she heard it open. "He just got back with breakfast for me. I didn't even have to go downstairs. I promise you, I'm okay. Don't worry about me. I'm going to take it easy today. You can look for more beautiful photos tomorrow. Uh, tell Bea and the kids I said hi."

"Okay, sweetheart. You take care of yourself."

"I love you, Grandmother."

"I love you more."

Cari ended the call and joined Bob over on the sofa. He had a plate full of raspberry scones, whipped butter, fresh fruit, a small metal pitcher, and a carafe of what she hoped was coffee.

"Please tell me that's coffee and I'll love you forever."

"Well, I'm in luck because that's exactly what it is. I put the little package of honey in my pocket and this little pitcher has the milk in it."

Bob grabbed two mugs from the side table and brought them over. He filled them both with coffee leaving a little space for Cari's extras in one mug. She smiled at him.

"Thank you for pampering me."

Bob put his arm around her and squeezed. "Of course. How are you feeling? How was the shower? How—"

"Easy there, big fella. One question at a time." Cari laughed. "Well, I just laughed and it didn't make my headache any worse. The shower was great, though I tried to replay what happened and remember something about the boat, but I couldn't. I felt like the Coast Guard people were disappointed with my responses yesterday."

"Hey, you can't tell them what you don't know. Was that your grandmother on the phone earlier?"

"Yeah, she was pretty shocked to hear about the concussion. She said she didn't know what she was going to do with me. I told her not to worry. I'm so much better today than yesterday."

"That's great. What do you feel up for today?"

"I don't know. Imagining other people seeing me like this is sort of horrifying. I wouldn't have called myself vain, but…I look terrible. Can I just hide in the room all day?"

"That's totally fine. I don't have any reservations and even if I did, we aren't going to jeopardize your health because of some easily rescheduled plans," he reassured her.

"Thank you. I'm sorry for spoiling this trip. I'll try to stop being a trouble magnet."

He laughed. "You're not a trouble magnet."

She smiled. "Did you say something about me looking at a photo array today? Is there an update on that?"

"Yes and no. I did say that, but I haven't heard any more about it."

"Do you think we could move it to tomorrow? I mean, I don't want to delay the investigation, but my headache is still a dull ache even with ibuprofen."

"One day isn't going to kill the case. When I take the breakfast dishes down, I'll let Aunt Lydia know you need more time."

Bob's phone buzzed. He quickly checked the screen, then pushed it back into his pocket. Cari watched his face and saw the familiar cloud settle over it.

"Is everything okay?"

He blinked. "Uh, yeah, just, uh…nothing to worry about."

She frowned, but decided not to be nosy. "These scones are even better than the blueberry ones from the first morning. I wish I was better at baking and I'd learn how to make them."

"Maybe Aunt Lydia would share the recipe with us and we could give it a try when we get back to New York. They are *really* good," he paused. "Say, have you heard from Genevieve?"

"Not since…uh, whenever I talked to her last." Cari grinned sheepishly. "Maybe I'll try to call her later when it's closer to her lunch hour. I don't even know if she gets a lunch break, but it's worth a shot."

Bob's phone buzzed again, but this time he didn't look at it. Cari wondered who was texting him. She grabbed another scone and tried to pretend like she hadn't heard it. She took a bite of the scone just as his phone buzzed a third time. Bob ran his fingers through his short hair but still didn't take out his phone. She felt awkward, like she was keeping him from something. She decided to just ask.

"Do you need to get—"

His phone vibrated with a longer tone, which Cari knew meant it was an incoming call. He rolled his eyes and pulled the phone out of his pocket.

"Hello? I'm sorry…yes. I'm not…okay. I'll call you back."

Cari continued nibbling on her scone and waited for him to explain. Her knee bounced as she tried to dispel some of her nervous energy. Bob slipped the phone back in his pocket and grabbed the last scone.

"Okay if I eat this?"

Cari blinked. She couldn't believe he was pretending like the phone call hadn't just happened. "Yeah, go for it. I'm already on my second one."

Bob gulped down the rest of his coffee. "I'm going to grab a quick shower. Do you need anything first?"

She started to shake her head no and thought better of it. "Nope. I'm perfectly content with the rest of my coffee."

Bob grabbed some clothing from his suitcase and went to the bathroom. Cari took another drink of coffee and got up to get her phone. Maybe she could send Genevieve a text and find out when they could chat later.

Hey, Gen. Got a minute?

The three dots appeared, indicating she was responding.

Sure, but just text. I can't talk right now. Is this about the break-in?

Did Alex tell you?

Yeah. Any update?

Not really. I haven't thought about it. I got a concussion yesterday.

What? Did you startle another burglar?

No. Long story. Hit my head on a kayak.

Tripped?

Cari sighed and tried to retell the story succinctly over text, but Gen texted again before she could formulate her response.

Wait. Could this be related to the break-in?

What? I don't see how.

Just seems weird, but gotta go. I'll try to call later.

Cari set her phone on the coffee table and took another drink of coffee. She hadn't considered the two events to be related at all, but maybe the concussion was clouding her thought processes. She jumped when the bathroom door swung open. Bob was dressed in his usual khaki pants and polo shirt. She smiled at him.

"I need to make a phone call. I'll be back. I'll lock the door behind me."

He left their room. Cari watched in dismay. *Why was he being so secretive? Was it Contessa?*

* * * * *

Lydia eyed Jack and Margie. Her sister-in-law was always looked polished and put together. Her straight, reddish-brown hair was clasped behind her head and her jewelry complemented her outfit perfectly. Margie had just spoken with Bob about bringing Cari down to meet them. Lydia didn't want to interfere, but wished her sister-in-law would give him some space. Before she could find the right words, her brother spoke up.

"Lyd, you said the sheriff was bringing over a photo array this morning?" he asked.

"Huh? Oh, yes. They're going to call me when they're about to be on their way. Bob said Cari agreed to look at it even though she didn't see the man's face."

"Well, you never know," Margie commented. "Oh, look. Here's Bob now."

Lydia looked up to see Bob striding across the dining room. He didn't look happy. She smiled, hoping to ease the tension in the room. Margie stood up.

"Bob! It's so great to see you," she exclaimed as she gave him a hug.

"You too, Mom…Dad," he said, shaking his dad's hand after hugging his mom. "Listen, I know you're excited to meet Cari, but she's still pretty tired. Her headache hasn't gone away yet and her face is really bruised."

"We don't care about how she looks, Bob. We won't say anything. We just want to meet her. After all we've heard about her…and you didn't bring her home at Christmas last year. I only know her from the social media posts she tags you in!"

"Mom…" Bob started.

116

"Margie, give the boy a break. He looks exhausted. We'll get to meet her. Just give her some time," Jack rebuked her.

Bob turned to Lydia. "Aunt Lydia, I told Cari I'd check with you about the photo array. Like I said, she's not feeling the greatest and doesn't want to see anyone today. Do you think they could hold off until tomorrow?"

"That is completely understandable. She does not need to add any extra stress to her body or brain right now." She turned to her brother. "Jack, why don't you come by my office after you finish your breakfast? I'm going to give Deputy Yarrow a call, then we can look at the security company quotes."

Jack nodded. "I'm basically finished. I can go with you now. Margie?"

"I'm going to enjoy the rest of my coffee while I stare at the lake. I'll meet you in the room later." She looked at Bob. "Call me when you're ready for us to meet Cari."

Bob nodded and stepped back so Lydia could get up from her seat. "I'm going to go check on Cari. Mom, I promise, as soon as she's feeling better, I will introduce you."

Lydia watched Bob walk away. She nodded to Jack and he pushed back from the table. Once inside her office, she walked around to the other side of the desk and found the phone number for the deputy. She punched it into her desk phone and waited for him to answer while Jack took a seat in one of the empty chairs.

"Deputy Yarrow speaking."

"This is Lydia Fairchild. I'm calling about the photo array."

"Great, I was just about to leave with it, assuming now is a good time?"

"I have some bad news. Cari has a pretty bad headache and doesn't feel like seeing anyone today. From the sound of it, she plans to spend the day in her room resting."

"I'm sorry to hear that, but I get it. My brother got a concussion in high school football and it took him a week before he was ready to go back to school. I'll bring it by tomorrow instead. No problem."

"Thank you. Bob seemed pretty confident that she would feel up to it by then."

"Just give me a call in the morning and we'll make a plan. Take care. In the meantime, I'll see if I can find anything else about the guy. We might try to pick him up if my boss thinks we have enough evidence here. I'll keep you posted."

"Thanks, deputy. I appreciate it."

Lydia hung up the phone and then pulled her personal cell phone out of her apron pocket. Rather than calling him and possibly waking Cari up, she sent a quick text to let him know Deputy Yarrow could wait on the photo array.

Lydia motioned to Jack to join her in front of the computer. He stood up and pushed his chair over to face the monitor. She frowned as it scuffed along the floor.

"By all means, make yourself at home," she admonished him.

"What?" he followed her eyes to the scrape marks on the hardwood floor. "Sorry. Maybe it will buff out. Margie can fix it. Let's look at those quotes."

* * * * *

Cari heard the key in the lock and looked up to see Bob. Even though he was smiling as he walked into their room, she could see the tension in his steps. Some vacation this was turning out to be.

"Everything okay? I'm sorry to keep asking. It's none of my business."

His shoulders dropped and he grimaced, though Cari suspected he thought he was smiling. "You don't have to be sorry. It's nothing. It's just…well, it's nothing."

Clearly nothing, Cari thought.

She took the last gulp of her coffee and set the mug on the table. "Did I hear you mention a game room earlier? Maybe we could work a puzzle together."

"If you don't think it will be too hard on your eyes, sure. Let me refresh my coffee and we'll head that way. Um..." he paused.

"Yes?"

"Never mind."

She started to press him to say more, but decided to let it go. "Do you think you could bring the puzzle up here? Is that against the rules?"

"I'm sure it's fine. Aunt Lydia won't care at all," he assured her.

He refilled his coffee mug and set the carafe back on the tray. "I will take the rest of our dishes back to the kitchen and get a puzzle on my way back."

"Sounds like a plan."

Cari stood up slowly and decided she could officially check dizziness off of her list of symptoms. Now if she could just get rid of the headache. Thankfully, the pain medication was keeping it at bay for the moment. She would know in a few hours if it was gone for good. She watched Bob open the door with one hand while balancing the tray in the other.

"You're pretty good with that tray. Did you ever work as a waiter?"

She could see his ears redden from behind. "Yes, uh, I was a waiter here a couple summers during high school. Um, that's how I met Contessa."

Cari gulped and was grateful to be behind him rather than face-to-face. She decided to ignore the reference to Contessa. "Did your whole family spend their summers out here?"

"My parents would come visit, but dad couldn't stay away from his job for too long. It's pretty easy to get here from Chicago, so

119

they came several weekends," he paused. "I'll be right back. Do you need anything? Water? More coffee?" he asked.

"I should probably say yes to water."

"See you in a minute."

Cari got up and walked over to the bed. She hadn't been awake for more than two hours, but she was suddenly feeling sleepy again. Maybe she could just take a short nap while Bob was fetching the puzzle. As she lay down, her mind drifted back to Bob's mention of Contessa. He seemed to be almost embarrassed of his relationship with her. Cari rolled through his words again and again, but was soon fast asleep.

* * * * *

Bob found a 500-piece puzzle that didn't look too hard. It was a view of the lake with sailboats in every color. It looked like one Cari would enjoy. He cringed as he remembered the look on Cari's face when he mentioned Contessa. He struggled with how to explain her to Cari. They'd had a little fling the last summer Bob worked at The Boarding House. Contessa had been a waitress alongside him and a romance of sorts sparked. He was awkward as a teen and had been easily ensnared by the lovely young woman's attention. Not wanting to lose her affection, he'd paid for everything they did together that summer and she had let him without saying a word. After returning to college, he tried texting her a few times and even calling her once, but she never responded. He was still embarrassed with how he'd let her manipulate him. He knew he should explain all of it to Cari, but he hated how foolish it made him look. He sighed and tucked two water bottles under his arm. He hadn't thought of Contessa in years and wished he could just erase that part of his past.

He picked up the puzzle with his free hand and climbed up the stairs to the main floor. He knew she didn't like taking it easy, but hoped Cari would give her brain time to heal from the trauma yesterday. Tomorrow, they could go on the lighthouse tour and maybe he could find just the right place to propose.

He reached their room and opened the door. Cari was sound asleep on the bed. He smiled and set the puzzle on the nightstand. They could start it later if she felt like it. He walked over to the sofa and put the two waters on the coffee table. He wanted to look at the overview of the lighthouse tour, so he pulled out his phone.

He'd made the reservation over a month ago and while it wasn't his first plan for the proposal, it would still be romantic. The tour included a ferry ride around the Apostle Islands and stopped at a few of the lighthouses along the way. At the final stop, you could climb to the top of the lighthouse on Specter Island and see all of Lake Superior. It was a fantastic view. A text popped up on the screen from his mom.

How is Cari feeling?

He rolled his eyes before responding. She is asleep.

Oh. I'm sorry she got hurt, Bob. I hope she feels better soon.

Thx.

He put the phone away and reached for his backpack. He'd brought a book along even though he wasn't sure he'd have time to read it. Glancing over at Cari, he realized he might have time for more than one book. He pulled out the book and started reading where he'd left off on the plane. He'd barely turned one page when he heard Cari yawn.

He smiled at her. "You're awake!"

She stretched her arms over her head and yawned again. "Yeah, sorry. How long have I been sleeping?"

He looked at his watch. It hadn't even been an hour since he'd left with the breakfast dishes. "Seriously, you don't need to be sorry. It's good to rest, especially when you have a concussion. To answer your question, it's been about forty-five minutes."

"Did you find a puzzle for us to do?"

He pointed at the nightstand. "I thought you might like all the colors in that one."

"Oh, it's so pretty. Are you ready to start it?"

"Bring it on over. I got you some water too." He grabbed a bottle and loosened the lid for her.

"Perfect. I'm going to take some of the Tylenol the nurse gave me yesterday and then I'll join you."

Bob watched as she rifled through her messenger bag. She pulled out one of the sample pouches from the urgent care nurse and walked over to the coffee table for the water. She took a sip and then put the pill in her mouth and gulped down some more water.

"Hopefully, that will do the trick. At least the room doesn't spin when I stand up any more. Progress."

* * * * *

Lydia sat next to Jack and watched him scroll through the quotes from the two security companies. He had a yellow legal pad in front of him and was jotting down notes in two columns. Margie had returned to their room to read a book, though Lydia suspected she was working up her nerve to find Bob and Cari.

"The first company included cameras at every entrance with digital recording service. They also have motion detectors for after-hours, which will activate the interior cameras. They'll install sensors on every door and all the windows in the common areas."

"What about the windows in the guest rooms? People open those at night sometimes. I don't want to inadvertently set off the alarm system because someone wants some fresh air while they sleep."

"It doesn't look like they included sensors for the guest rooms."

"What if someone tries to break-in through a window that's open?"

"All the guest rooms are on the second or third floor. It's pretty typical not to have alarm sensors on above-ground windows in hotels and other lodging places."

"Okay, continue."

"The second quote has fewer cameras—none for the interior. Their window alarms include glass-breakage—"

"But I just replaced all the windows!" Lydia complained

Jack looked at her pointedly before answering. She recognized his expression from childhood and realized he was growing impatient. "The windows don't have to be replaced again. They add sensors to them which will sound an alarm if the glass breaks."

"It all sounds really expensive."

"Both systems come with an app you can use to monitor the status of the building from anywhere. The front door will have a programmable lock you can activate from your phone."

"Well, what do you think? Which one is cheaper?"

"Cheaper isn't necessarily the best choice. What will make you—*and your guests* feel safe?"

Lydia sighed. "I don't think I can afford either one."

"Margie and I can help. This doesn't have to fall on you. I know you are the business owner, but we're still family. I would hate to see you lose this place as much as you would hate to lose it."

"I think we need to do the one with the glass sensors then. I need to put a stop to these break-ins. I'm not sure an alarm system will do that, but at least it might make the intruder think twice before trying again."

"I'll give them a call," Jack said, picking up the desk phone receiver.

"No, I need to do it. They'll need payment information and you don't have any of that."

"They won't need that yet. They will run a credit check to be sure you can cover the payments. I still have your social memorized—"

"You have got to be kidding me. If my identity is ever stolen, I know who to talk to first. Fine, make the call. I'm going to go check in with the housekeeping staff. Let me know if you need anything."

She got up and left Jack in her office. Asking for help was going to take some getting used to, but she was glad to have her brother by her side. Hopefully, they could get things back on track soon.

* * * * *

Cari sifted through another pile of pieces and pulled out more edges. They missed a few the first time and were also short one corner piece. She was starting to wonder if the community puzzle didn't have all five hundred pieces to begin with. They'd been sorting through pieces for about half an hour, but Bob had been on his phone at least half the time responding to texts. She could tell he was getting increasingly uncomfortable and wished he would talk to her. He hadn't been himself in days; part of her worried this vacation wasn't going the way he'd hoped. Maybe their relationship wasn't as strong as she thought. She realized she was staring off into space and looked at Bob. He was fidgeting with his watch. She decided to just ask him what was wrong.

"Is everything okay, Bob?"

"Uh, it's nothing. It's fine. Don't worry about it," he said quickly.

"I know I'm not totally with it today, but I can still tell that something is bothering you. What's going on? Please talk to me."

Bob ran a hand over his head and sighed. "I'm sorry. I have a confession to make."

Cari felt the color drain from her face. *Contessa. He must have—*

"It's not *that* bad," he laughed nervously. "It's my parents. They arrived last night after Aunt Lydia called Dad about all the struggles with the business. My mom is beside herself wanting to meet you. I told her you didn't feel up for visitors and you're recovering from a concussion..."

Cari exhaled. "Your parents? That was not what I expected you to say. Thank you for keeping my best interests at heart, but I would love to meet your parents...I was hoping not to look like the loser of a boxing match when that happened."

"No one could ever call you a loser. I'm sorry for springing it on you. There's a chance my mom might just *happen* to come up here at some point today. I would rather you be expecting it than caught off-guard."

"Thank you." Cari pulled out her phone and looked at her face again using the selfie feature of her camera. "Well, this has not gotten better," she said tracing a circle around her face.

"I told her you weren't up for meeting people today. Hopefully, she can show some restraint."

"Let's hope your aunt can keep them entertained, but it will be fine either way. Now, let's see if we can get this puzzle together."

Chapter 10

C ari yawned herself awake and realized it was morning. She gently pressed her fingers to the bandage on her forehead and was relieved not to have searing pain in her temples. She did have a headache, but it was a dull pain compared to what she had experienced the day before.

Somehow, Bob had managed to keep his mother from "popping by" yesterday. He'd gone up and down the stairs with food and dishes and water so many times, she lost count. He was probably exhausted from that. She noticed her running shoes across the room and pouted. She probably shouldn't be doing any running for a few days, which meant she wasn't going to talk Bob into doing any running on his own either. They would have to make up for it when they got back to New York.

She tried to slip out of bed quietly, but the floorboard creaked when she stood up. Bob groaned and rolled over to look at her. He blinked the sleep out of his eyes and then smiled.

"How is the princess in the tower doing today?" he teased.

She feigned hurt. "Um, rude. And I'm feeling much better. I still have a bit of a headache, but nothing ibuprofen can't fix. I haven't looked in the mirror yet. Do I still look like a battered woman?"

He tilted his head in thought. "I think I see some improvement."

"You better not be lying. I'm going to take a shower. I'll check myself out and see if I feel up for breakfast downstairs or not."

She grabbed a change of clothing and stepped into the bathroom. She took a deep breath before looking in the mirror. It couldn't be as bad as yesterday. She slowly turned and looked at her reflection. She pursed her lips. Well, it wasn't as bad as yesterday, but it wasn't good either. She could probably cover some of it up with makeup.

"Breakfast will be upstairs again!" she called out to Bob.

"Scones?" He hollered back.

"Works for me."

At least her hair wasn't too unsightly today. It helped that she literally stayed in the room all day the day before; no wind exposure to frizz out her curls. She decided to forego washing her hair and grabbed the complimentary shower cap from the bathroom counter.

Bob wasn't in the room when she came out of the bathroom. She figured he'd run downstairs to get their scones and hopefully a full carafe of coffee. She checked her phone and saw he'd texted just that. She went back into the bathroom to do her makeup. She was definitely going to meet Bob's parents today and hoped they wouldn't be shocked by her appearance. She cringed. She also had to meet with the deputy and look at the photo array. She brushed on some more powder and looked herself over again.

"I'm back!" Bob called out from the room.

"I'll be right out. I'm trying to cover up my wounds with some makeup."

She scooped her supplies up and tossed them back in her travel bag. Bob was pouring coffee when she stepped out of the bathroom. He looked up and gave her a smile.

"I would never guess that you lost to the heavyweight champion in the fight of the year two nights ago."

"Shut it."

"I'm just kidding. You look great. Have some coffee and a scone. Lydia said Deputy Yarrow will be here in half an hour. I figured you felt up for it. I hope that's okay."

"Yeah, I don't want to put it off any more than I already have. Hopefully, they can find this guy and keep him from terrorizing Lydia's business."

"Great. By the way, my dad is working with Aunt Lydia in her office right now and I saw my mom head out for a walk while I was downstairs. We could head down to the game room to return this puzzle without being seen yet."

Cari smiled. "Stealth mode. I like it. You grab the food tray and I'll take care of the doors. Maybe we can start another puzzle while we wait for the deputy to arrive."

* * * * *

Lydia drummed her fingers on her desk. The deputy should be here any minute. She didn't know why she was nervous to look at the lineup, or photo array, or whatever it was called. She just wanted to be past all of it. She pulled out her phone and started scrolling through the news headlines to distract herself.

"It looks like the sheriff's deputy just pulled up," Jack said, motioning toward the window.

Lydia looked up to see Deputy Yarrow getting out of his cruiser. "Great. How is it coming with the security company stuff?"

"I was able to talk them out of the installation fee yesterday. We should hear from them about an installation date soon. They won't send anyone out today since it's the weekend, but hopefully they can get us on the schedule tomorrow. I'll give them a call and see if I can't speed things along. They always have customer and technical support people available."

"Okay, keep me posted."

Lydia left Jack in her office and crossed the lobby to welcome Deputy Yarrow inside. He was carrying a manila folder in his left hand. She stepped back to let him enter the building.

"Welcome back, Deputy. Thanks for making the drive over. How does this usually work?"

"Well, I'd like to do this in your office or another more private area if possible. It's better if you have a quiet place to review the photos."

Lydia tapped her chin. "My brother is in my office right now making arrangements with the security company, but we have another place that should work. We stopped having guest rooms on the ground floor a few years ago and converted the suite down here into a conference room or private dining area. I thought you wanted to show the array to my nephew's girlfriend first, though."

"It doesn't matter who looks at it first. You're here and ready to go, so I might as well start with you."

Lydia nodded. "Right this way."

* * * * *

Cari gently rubbed her eyes and sighed. She could feel the headache coming back. So much for being symptom free.

"Is your head bothering you?" Bob asked her with concern.

She closed her eyes and opened them slowly. "I wish I could say no, but I think the ibuprofen I took this morning is starting to wear off."

"You can alternate Tylenol and ibuprofen. Do you want me to go upstairs and grab it for you?"

She smiled as she pulled a sample pouch from her pocket. "Thank you, but I planned ahead and brought it with me. I am going to take a break from the puzzle though."

Bob looked around the room, his gaze settling on the old photo albums. "Being here brings back so many memories. We used to celebrate Christmas down here. My grandfather would regale us with stories from the past after we opened gifts."

Cari was intrigued. "What kind of stories?"

Bob chuckled. "Well, there was one he told every year. I think we all had it memorized word for word at one point. Let's see if I can remember it." He stood up and walked over to the shelving with the albums.

"All these old guest books…he would pull the oldest one off the shelf and flip to the front where some of the first tenants of the original boarding house signed their names."

"Wait, those are guest books? I thought they were photo albums!"

"Oh no, these are all the guest books." He bent down and ran his finger along the bindings. "Weird. I can't find the oldest one; it's easy to spot because the spine has a big dent in it. Maybe Lydia decided to put it somewhere safer, for posterity."

"Well, let's hear this story already." Cari pushed her chair back from the table and crossed her legs.

"Okay. Let me think. Not long after Grandfather Willoughby opened the boarding house, a group of five men came through town looking for rooms to rent for one night. They were on their way to California, hoping to strike it rich in gold. One of the men rose earlier than his friends and shared a cup of coffee with the man of the house. He had a sweetheart back in Pennsylvania who he planned to return to after a successful mining trip.

"He had promised this young woman he'd bring home his riches so they could marry and start a life together. His comrades were single and had no plans to make the long trip back home. They were going to start a new life in California with their shares of the gold."

"Oh, wow, it's like a love story. How sweet!" Cari exclaimed.

"Well, keep listening. There's more. A few weeks after the five friends set off from Wisconsin for California, this young man returned, late in the night. He was dirty and hungry and frantic to get inside. Willoughby had taken a liking to him. He welcomed him into the house and offered him food and water. The man said he couldn't stay. Their search for gold hadn't been as plentiful as he'd hoped. Splitting their findings five ways barely left him with enough to make it back to Pennsylvania, but he missed his sweetheart and couldn't stay away any longer. He couldn't fathom the idea of returning to his bride empty-handed and penniless, so he decided to double-cross his friends."

"Oh, no! That's terrible," Cari said in shock.

"I know, right? It was risky enough to travel so far from home with no guarantee of finding gold but to steal from your own friends? Pretty bad."

Cari started to respond when Bob's phone buzzed with an incoming text. He pulled it out and looked at it. She expected him to stay silent and slip the phone back into his pocket, but he spoke up.

"Well, it seems story time is over. The deputy is here and ready for you to look at the lineup, if you feel up to it."

"Of course, though I'm not sure if it will do any good. I never saw his face."

"Deputy Yarrow will meet you at the landing. According to my dad, Aunt Lydia gave him a conference room to use."

"Your dad? I just assumed your aunt would have texted you."

Bob frowned. "Yeah, that is strange. I guess we'll find out what's going on once we get up there."

* * * * *

Cari followed Bob back up the stairs. When they reached the landing, she saw an older version of Bob standing outside Lydia's office. His hair was mostly grey and cut close to his scalp. He smiled when he saw them and waved them over. Cari held back a giggle when she saw Bob's dad was also wearing khakis and a polo shirt. Bob's dad was a few inches taller than him, but had the same blue eyes and kind smile. She relaxed her shoulders and smiled back.

"Bob, good to see you again," the man said as he shook Bob's hand before turning to Cari. "And you must be Cari. I'm so sorry to hear about your accident. How are you feeling?"

"I've been better. I'd say 'you should see the other guy', but I'm pretty sure the kayak is totally fine."

"Well, it's great to meet you," he paused. "Deputy Yarrow asked me to take you over to the conference room to look at the photo array one at a time. He doesn't want one person to influence another's response."

Bob nodded. "Makes sense. Cari, do you want to go first?"

"Sure. Nice to meet you, uh, Mr. Hursley."

The man stuck out his hand. "Please, call me Jack. The conference room is just around the corner."

Cari shook his hand and followed him down the hallway. He opened the first door on the right for her. Deputy Yarrow was sitting on the corner of the table and stood up when she entered. He had a manila folder in his right hand that he was tapping against his left.

"Ms. Turnlyle. Thanks for coming up," he cringed. "They told me you were in an accident, but, wow! I didn't realize…"

"It looks pretty bad, huh?"

He grimaced. "It looks like it hurts. Anyway, I've got the photo array right here. I know you said you didn't see his face, but we'd still like you to take a look."

"Certainly."

Deputy Yarrow opened the folder and pulled out a single sheet of paper. The page was laminated and had two rows of images, with three in each row. He kept his hand in the center of the page.

"I have my body camera on—actually, it's been on this whole time…uh, it's always on when I'm wearing it. Anyway, it will record your response to the photos. Take your time looking at each one. You're welcome to pick it up too."

He removed his hand from the page and Cari slowly picked it up. Each of the six men in the images had dark brown hair and varying amounts of facial hair. She looked at each face and thought back to three days ago and her encounter with the intruder. She shook her head in disappointment.

"I'm sorry. I never saw his face. I wish I could be more helpful."

Yarrow smiled. "Don't worry about it. We knew it was a long shot. Could you ask Mr. Hursley, uh, the younger Mr. Hursley, to come in now?"

Cari almost nodded her head yes before remembering about her concussion. "I'll send him right in. Thanks."

She opened the door and stepped aside so Bob could take his turn. She could tell the two men had been having a discussion before she opened the door. She wondered what she had interrupted. *And where was Lydia?*

"Any luck?" Jack asked her.

"No. I only saw the man from behind. As much as I wanted to be able to identify someone on that page, I didn't have the slightest recollection of any of them."

"I think they were expecting that, right?"

"Yes, I told them the other day I didn't see his face, but I know they have to at least try to get an ID," she hesitated before continuing. "I was just wondering, where is Lydia?"

Jack pressed his lips together before answering. "Well, it turns out—"

Before he finished answering her question, Bob and Deputy Yarrow came out of the conference room. Yarrow had the folder back in his hand. Cari tried to read Bob's expression, but both he and Yarrow remained stoic.

Deputy Yarrow addressed Jack. "Could you get Ms. Fairchild to join us over here? I'd like to speak to everyone together."

Jack nodded in agreement. "I'll be right back."

Cari looked at the deputy in bewilderment. Clearly, she was missing part of the story here. Lydia hadn't seen the intruder at all, and she didn't think Bob had either. She didn't know if it was okay to ask him at this point or if she should wait until Yarrow told them more. She shifted her weight to her other hip and tapped her foot.

"Ms. Turnlyle, I can see you are confused. I'll explain in just a moment," Yarrow reassured her.

Jack and Lydia rounded the corner. Lydia was carrying a laptop; her face was flushed and she stared through Bob and Cari like they weren't even there. Jack had the guestbook she had signed a few days ago. Cari wished her brain would connect the dots faster; she couldn't figure out what the guestbook would tell them regarding the break-ins. She sighed and followed the group back into the conference room.

Jack spoke up. "Unless you need something from me, I'm going to get back to making the arrangements with the security company."

Yarrow waved him off. "Go right ahead. Thanks for your help...everyone else, please take a seat. I'm going to get Sheriff Maruthers on the line so we can bring her up to date."

Jack handed the guestbook to Yarrow and then retreated down the hallway. Cari felt Bob grab her hand and give it a quick squeeze before releasing it. They pulled out chairs from the opposite side of the table and sat down across from the deputy and Lydia. Lydia gingerly placed the laptop on the table and blinked a few times.

"I still can't believe...I just...how..." she stammered.

"Just one second while the sheriff picks up, please," Yarrow reminded her.

The sheriff's voice came in over the phone's speaker. "This is Sheriff Maruthers. What do you have for me, deputy?"

"I'm here with Mrs. Lydia Fairchild, Ms. Cari Turnlyle, and Mr. Bob Hursley. I shared the photo array with each of them separately. The latter two were unable to identify anyone from the array, but Mrs. Fairchild immediately recognized person four as one of her former guests."

"Right, and do those present confirm these statements by Deputy Yarrow?" Maruthers asked.

"State your name before responding, please," Yarrow interjected.

"Bob Hursley, I concur."

"Cari Turnlyle, I also concur."

"Lydia Fairchild, I, uh, yes, I recognized the man in photo four."

"Thank you, deputy. After Mrs. Fairchild's identification, she went to review her records of when this person was an occupant of The Boarding House, correct?" Sheriff Maruthers asked.

"That's correct," the deputy responded.

"Okay, Mrs. Fairchild, do you have your records with you?"

"Yes," Lydia spoke up, but her voice was barely above a whisper. She swallowed and cleared her throat. "Yes, ma'am. I have the guestbook and the records with me."

"Our department identified the palm print on the basement door and the palm print on the balcony railing as belonging to one Mr. Lucien Merrick. Mrs. Fairchild, I understand you are not familiar with that name."

"That's correct. My guest was a Mr. Jasper Benavidez, but the man in the photo is the same man. I'm certain of that...I just can't believe he's behind all the break-ins. He was here when the second break-in occurred—"

135

"Aunt Lydia, doesn't that make it more believable?" Bob interrupted.

"No! He was so helpful. The broken glass…he helped me clean it up and he helped me tape cardboard over the window to keep the bugs out. He was so nice. I just can't believe it was all an act."

"I understand, Mrs. Fairchild. He seemed like a Good Samaritan," Sheriff Maruthers said gently. "Can you give me the address Mr. Benavidez gave you when he registered as a guest?"

"Yes, just one second." Lydia opened the laptop and hit a few keys. "Here it is. Jasper Benavidez, party of one. Thirteen Lazy Brook Lane, Danison, Minnesota. Do you need the zip code?"

"No, Danison only has one zip for the whole town. That address differs from the one on his Lucien Merrick driver's license, but I'd still consider it a local address. I'm going to run a search on your Mr. Benavidez with that address. We'll put in a call over to the neighboring county in Minnesota and see if they can spare two officers to pick him up from the address he listed while we check out the Wisconsin one that pulled up with his prints. We'll bring him in for questioning. Do you have any questions, Mrs. Fairchild?" Sheriff Maruthers asked.

"No, I mean, maybe. If he confesses or is found guilty, will he have to pay me back for the damages? The broken windows and so forth?"

"It's really too early to discuss repercussions. If he doesn't have the money, it will make recompense more difficult too. Let's take it one step at a time."

Deputy Yarrow spoke up. "I will get copies of Mrs. Fairchild's records for evidence and be back at the station in half an hour."

"See you then. Hopefully, we'll have this all wrapped up soon. Thanks for your cooperation."

Cari heard the line click indicating the call had ended. Yarrow put the phone back in his pocket and stood up from the table. Lydia looked up from her seat at him.

"Should I just print this registration form for you? Do you want a copy of the guestbook page too? He signed it as well."

"Yeah, let's do both. Do you have a printer in your office?"

Lydia nodded and got up from the table after closing her laptop. "I sent the form over to the printer already. It's wireless, however that works. We can make a copy of the other in my office."

Deputy Yarrow turned to Cari and Bob. "I'm sorry to spring all this information on you. I wasn't expecting your aunt to recognize someone in the array. It all came together rather quickly. I just needed you to be present to verify the results of the photo array."

"Not much of a burglar, I guess," Bob quipped.

"He was persistent, I'll give him that. He even paid for a room for a couple nights and then faked a break-in." Yarrow responded.

"I was going to ask you about that. I noticed some broken glass in the bushes outside the window in the dining room. If the intruder had come from the outside, the glass should have fallen inside when the window was hit."

"That's right. Your aunt mentioned you're a crime tech. Occasionally, you might see a piece or two fall back towards the break instead of away from it, but I found several shards under the bush. He must have broken the window from the inside."

"But why break it at all if he was already here legally?" Cari asked.

The deputy tilted his head in contemplation. "That's a great question. There may be more to this than it seems. I'll be in touch. Thanks again for your help."

Yarrow shook their hands and hurried down the hallway after Lydia. Cari got up from her seat and followed Bob to the doorway. After looking behind the doors for the correct light switch, he finally found it on the outside wall.

"How are you feeling?" he asked her.

Cari gently pushed on the bandage on her forehead. "Not too bad, actually."

"It's basically lunchtime. Are you hungry?"

"Now that you mention it, I am really hungry…" Her shoulders drooped. "I look terrible though. I mean, my eyes looked like I took one to both sockets when I looked in the mirror this morning."

Bob pulled her into a hug. "Hey, you are beautiful. I understand if you're feeling self-conscious about the bruises, though. I could go pick up some sandwiches or fish tacos for us?"

She sighed. She hated feeling like she was high maintenance, but she also didn't want to spend the day dodging stares from everyone on the street. "No, I'll go with you. Maybe some vitamin D will speed up the healing process."

* * * * *

Lydia opened the door to her office and slid into a chair across from Jack. He was on the phone, presumably with the security company and she didn't want to interrupt him. She could feel her hands trembling again and squeezed the laptop and guestbook tighter. She took a deep breath and set the two items on her desk before remembering she needed to copy the guestbook for the deputy. She grabbed the book and went over to the small copier. As she waited for it to scan the correct page, she replayed the interaction with Lucien Merrick or Jasper Benavidez or whatever the man's name was. Had he been toying with her? Did he laugh at her naivete after he returned to his room?

"Earth to Lydia…" Jack broke into her thoughts.

Lydia ran a hand over her face. "What? Oh. Sorry. I was just having a little pity party. What's up?"

"I've gotten everything arranged with the security company. They're going to come out Monday at ten to start installing the system. They ran a credit check, which you passed, um…Lyd?" Jack stood up and came around the desk.

Lydia felt the panic rising up in her again. "I know. You don't have to say it. My credit isn't great. I can barely pay the property taxes each year. We drained most of our savings with Harvey's medical bills and decided to mortgage the business. I'm sorry I didn't tell you. I was too ashamed."

Jack grabbed her hand. "Hey, don't beat yourself up. You did what you needed to do."

Lydia bit her lip. "You don't sound surprised about the mortgage."

"It came up during the credit check, Lyd. I'm sorry. I didn't mean to find out behind your back."

"No, don't apologize. I should have told you before. I guess I thought I could get everything turned around and back on track."

Jack nodded with understanding. "I get it. I can't imagine how hard all this has been. Can I look at your mortgage paperwork? Maybe we can refinance it and get you a better rate."

Lydia blinked back the tears filling her eyes. "Refinance? With what? You saw it yourself; my credit is not what it once was."

"Let me just look at it, Lyd. What will it hurt? Margie and I could co-sign—"

"No! You don't need to take on my troubles. Don't ruin your credit by getting involved with my troubles."

"Think about it. Let me at least look at your paperwork, okay?"

Lydia nodded. "It's in the filing cabinet. I'll get it out for you."

Jack gave her hand another squeeze. "Lydia, look at me. It's going to be okay. You're not going to lose this place. I promise."

Chapter 11

C ari wiped the grease off her chin and smiled up at Bob. They had ordered fish tacos to go from one of the local diners. They brought the tacos and bottled water to the end of a pier and commandeered a bench for a pseudo picnic.

"This is nice. Great idea, Bob."

"How is your head feeling? It's been a few hours since you took anything, right?" Bob asked with concern.

"Yeah, I guess it has been three or four hours now. Maybe the headache is going away for good. I'm not going to take off these sunglasses and see how my eyes react to the sunlight though. It's definitely too bright out here for that."

Bob wiped his hands on a napkin. "Man, what a day…what a week really. I thought we could come here to relax and we just keep getting hit with one thing after another."

"What day is it, anyway? I've lost track. Is it Sunday? I thought I might give Gen a call and see how the training program is going."

Bob grinned at her. "And throw out some theories of what you think is happening with the break-ins? See if she agrees with you?"

Cari smirked. "You know me too well. Should I put it on speakerphone?"

Bob laughed. "Not necessary. I brought a book to read. I'm planning to get some relaxing in today, one way or another."

Cari pulled out her phone and found Genevieve's number. Her friend picked up immediately.

"Hey Cari! Great to hear from you. How is Wisconsin? How is the concussion?"

"Thanks. Wisconsin is…mostly good, I think. The concussion is improving, I guess. They say it takes time; everyone is different, blah, blah, blah."

"Did they find the guy who caused it?" Genevieve asked with concern.

Cari hesitated. "I haven't heard anything. I mean, we didn't really see the guy or his boat. I'm not sure they have much to go on. The sheriff's office got a hit on the print from the intruder here, though."

"Give me a second. I can tell this is something I want to sit down to hear. And maybe take notes."

Cari heard her friend rummaging around. She waited for silence before launching into her stories.

"Okay, I'm ready. Spill."

"Let's see. Some guy has been breaking into the bed and breakfast for the last month. He was in our room when I got back from running a few days ago."

"Right. Alex told me about that when I spoke with him the other day. Did the guy break in again? Were you hurt?"

"Hey, chill. I'm fine. We've only been here for one of the break-ins and I did not get hurt during that excursion."

Genevieve sighed. "I'm listening. Let's hear the rest."

Cari told her about going kayaking and the speedboat and her subsequent concussion. She subconsciously ran a finger over her locket when she told her friend about getting stitches above her eye.

"The good news is, I think my headache is finally gone. Now I just look like I took a few fists to the face."

141

Genevieve groaned. "Ugh, Cari. You just seem to find trouble wherever you go. Now, tell me more about this intruder. Did the police come and take a report? Did they get any prints?"

"Whoa, slow down. Yes, Alex actually connected us with the county sheriff. She was one of his training officers back in the day."

"She isn't retired?"

Cari laughed. "That's what I said. No, she's not retired. Anyway, Bob's aunt couldn't remember who had come out to take reports from the earlier break-ins, so I reached out to Alex. He happened to know the sheriff out here and it's been a huge help. They did get a hit from two of the prints. It turns out they came from one of Lydia's former guests!"

"But, wouldn't a guest have left prints? That seems like a dead end."

"Except one of the prints was a palm print on the balcony in *our* room. We're on the third floor and this guy stayed on the second floor. He was only a guest for two days too. *AND* one of the break-ins happened the night he was a guest. He actually helped Lydia clean up the broken glass."

"What? Let me get this straight. This guy has broken in four times, once while he was already a guest? What has he stolen?"

"Nothing. Well, wait. Maybe a guestbook. I think I heard Lydia mention that. It's like the oldest guestbook from when this place was an actual boarding house in the 1800s."

"He's looking for something, but it's more than that. The break-ins are more than attempts to find it, they're also a scare tactic. He has another end-game here."

"I thought so too! I think there's much more going on than Lydia first suspected. Oh, I almost forgot. The guy gave a different address when he registered as a guest than he had listed on his driver's license. One address is in Minnesota and the other is in Wisconsin."

"What do you wanna bet that neither address is real?"

Cari felt the air rush out of her, but something told her Genevieve would be right. "I sure hope you're wrong. I think Lydia was hoping to put a stop to these break-ins now that they identified the guy."

"Keep me posted. I'm curious to know how this plays out."

"For sure. Tell me about you. How is the training program?"

Cari listened as Genevieve recalled the activities and exercises. It sounded like an intense program, but she could hear her friend's excitement. Bob's phone buzzed, distracting Cari from her phone call. She watched as he thumbed off a response and then put his phone back in his pocket. He drummed his fingers on his knees for a moment, then picked his book back up. Before he could open it, his phone buzzed again. He set the book aside and glanced her way.

"Hey, Gen, I'm sorry to cut this short, but I need to hang up. Call me again soon when you get the chance."

"Will do. Stay out of trouble over there. No more concussions, okay?"

Cari chuckled. "I'll do my best. Take care of yourself."

She ended the call and tilted her head at Bob. "What's up? Do we need to go back?"

Bob sighed. "My dad just texted. The sheriff's department struck out with the address in Wisconsin. It was an abandoned home. When they pulled the history on it, they found out no one has lived there in over a decade."

"Genevieve predicted the address would be a bust. I wish she'd been wrong."

"They did have some good news, well, kind of."

Cari leaned forward in anticipation. "Let's hear it."

"When they ran the name "Jasper Benavidez" through their system, they found another address."

Cari raised her eyebrows. "Who is this guy?"

* * * * *

Lydia took a sip of her iced tea and sighed. Margie had talked her into relaxing on the front porch for a bit while Jack looked over the mortgage paperwork. She really needed to get back inside and help with the laundry. They had two couples that checked out already today and three more coming in tomorrow. She'd reduced her housekeeping staff to weekdays only after last year's property tax increase. The beds weren't going to make themselves. She started to get up, but Margie raised her hand in protest.

"Sit back down, woman. You need to catch your breath. Enjoy your tea and the fresh air."

"I wish I could, Margie, but I have guest rooms to make up for tomorrow. I need to get the sheets and towels in the wash first. We had two checkouts today and I'm using at least one of those rooms tomorrow, so—"

"I already stripped the beds and got the sheets in the washer. Now, sit down and enjoy your tea." Margie commanded her.

Lydia's jaw dropped. "Margie, you didn't have to do that. This is my place to serve you."

"Not today it isn't. Drink up, dear."

"Did Jack tell you the sheriff's office called with another update?"

"He said they found a third alias or something?"

"A third address actually. I should probably go inside and call them to see if they have another update." She started to get up again, but Margie put her hand on her arm.

"Oh no you don't. You're not a detective. Sit down and drink your tea," she paused while Lydia settled back into her chair again. "Now, tell me about Cari. I still haven't gotten to meet her. I can't believe Jack beat me to it."

144

She smiled. "I haven't spent a lot of time with her. I've been too busy with everything going on. She seems really nice. I think she makes Bob happy."

Margie beamed. "I *know* she makes Bob happy. I can hear it in his voice every time he talks about her."

"You can see it in his eyes when he looks at her too. He's definitely in love with her." Lydia agreed.

"And so much better than that dreadful Contessa!" Margie growled.

Lydia chuckled. "Oh, that's a bit harsh. In fact, Contessa successfully operates her own bed and breakfast now. It's over in the neighboring town. I like to think that I was a good influence on her."

Margie pursed her lips before responding. "She treated Bob horribly and he just let her, but you're right. That was years ago. I'm sure she has grown up and matured since then."

Lydia nodded. "She is doing very well, as far as I can tell, but enough about her. I'm excited for you to meet Cari. I have found her to be charming and smart."

"I thought he brought her here for some sort of romantic proposal trip! Jack said she wasn't wearing a ring this morning though."

Lydia watched as Margie picked up her phone from her lap and thumbed off a text. She waited until her sister-in-law looked up before she spoke.

"Margie, you aren't texting Bob about his proposal, are you?" Lydia asked gently.

Margie's face reddened a bit. "I'm just checking in. This is step one to grandchildren, you know!"

"Well, I'm sure Bob has it under control," Lydia said slowly, hoping she wasn't overstepping boundaries by rebuking Margie.

"I know. I know. Oh, it's so hard to let them do things on their own, you know?" she asked with a grimace.

"I think there's been a few hiccups with his plans. As far as I know, he's still planning on proposing. Maybe he's doing it right now over lunch!" Lydia remarked.

Margie leaned forward and squinted into the sun. "Oh look, here they come now."

"Oh, now I see what you're really up to. You knew they would come back this way. I'm just a pawn in your game, huh?"

Margie grinned mischievously. "A girl's gotta do what a girl's gotta do."

Lydia watched as the young couple made their way up the sidewalk. She could see the edge of the bandage on Cari's face peeking out from behind her sunglasses. Bob was holding her hand and carrying a book. He didn't look exactly thrilled to see the two women sitting on the porch.

Margie stood up from her chair. "Bob! What an unexpected treat. Lydia and I were just enjoying some fresh air after lunch."

Bob gave her the side eye. "Hello, Mom. I don't believe that for a minute." He turned to Cari. "Cari, this is my mom, Margie Hursley. Mom, this is Cari."

Margie started to swoop in for a hug, but a stern look from Bob made her stop short. Lydia tried to hide the amusement from her face and was glad no one was looking her way.

"It's so wonderful to finally meet you. Sit down and chat with us for a moment."

Lydia watched Margie eyeing Cari's left hand. She could see Bob staring daggers at his mother in protest. Before she could think of something to say to distract Margie from overplaying her hand, Cari spoke up.

"Oh, we would love to, but Jack texted about the intruder. He has a third address?"

Margie looked at Bob and back to Cari. "I forgot you are somewhat of a sleuth. You two are like peas in a pod. Always tracking down clues, even when you're on vacation! Well, go ahead. Why don't we all eat dinner together this evening?"

Bob's face flushed. Lydia couldn't remember what he'd planned for that evening. "Why don't we plan on cocktails instead? Cari and I have reservations at the Lighthouse Restaurant tonight."

Margie's shoulders dropped. "Okay, but we really should eat one meal together while we're all here."

"I'll see what I can figure out. Does five o'clock work for cocktail hour?" Bob asked her.

Margie nodded.

Cari grabbed Margie's hand and gave it a squeeze. "It was lovely to meet you, Margie. See you in a few hours."

Lydia waited until the door was firmly closed behind them before speaking. "Well?"

"Well, what?" Margie asked her.

"Did that go as you'd planned?"

"Not exactly, but it's better than nothing. There's still no ring on that finger. What is that boy waiting for?"

"I really think he has it under control. I'm going to go check on Jack and move the laundry to the dryer."

"I'll take care of the laundry. You go help Jack get your mortgage straightened out."

* * * * *

Bob knocked on the door to Lydia's office as he opened it. They saw his dad sitting behind the desk and writing some figures on a legal pad. He looked up as they entered.

"Hey, Dad. What else did the sheriff say about the third address? Do they think this one will lead them to him?"

"Deputy Yarrow called Lydia. She put the call on speaker, so I could hear it. He said both addresses from before—the one in the guestbook and the one that came up with his prints—weren't valid residences."

"Right, you said one was an abandoned house?" Bob asked him.

"Yes, and the other wasn't even a house. It was a warehouse or something of the sort."

Cari spoke up. "What about the third address? Have they gone out to it yet?"

"It's another Minnesota address, so they put in a request to the other station as it's out of their jurisdiction. Their colleagues were a little put off from the last wild goose chase and suggested they research the address some before sending them out again."

"And?" Bob leaned in, awaiting his answer.

"It's a dry-cleaning business."

Cari was intrigued. "An active business? Not something that's out of business or dilapidated?"

"Oh no, it's an active business, but there's no place for someone to live there. They still don't know where this guy is."

"This isn't a dead end, though. I can look the business up…find a list of employees, financial records…" she trailed off as she thought about it.

"How? That surely isn't public information."

"I can log in to my LexisNexis account. The police can definitely get more information about the man or the business with a warrant, but I can get quite a bit and I don't need a warrant." She told him confidently.

Before Jack could respond, Lydia entered the office. "Who needs a warrant and for what?"

"Lydia! I was hoping you'd come by," Jack motioned for her to join him on the other side of the desk. "I've read through your paperwork. You have a really high rate on your mortgage. It's costing you a ton in interest right now. Almost none of your payment is going toward principle."

Bob interrupted. "Should we go? I don't want to intrude."

Lydia waved him off. "Nonsense. It's a *family* business. Jack, continue."

"I've looked around for lenders in your area. Of course, we'll have wait until Monday to get an appointment at your bank, but we can definitely get you a lower, fixed-rate mortgage. Your payment will go down. It won't change your property taxes, but it will lessen the financial strain."

"Did you look at the offer from that realtor guy?" Bob asked him.

Lydia's face reddened. "Oh, uh, I hadn't mentioned that…"

"Offer?" Jack asked in confusion.

"A local realtor claims to have an interested buyer. He brought by an offer earlier this week." Bob explained.

Lydia put up her hand to stop Jack from speaking. "Before you ask, no, the business is not for sale, it has never been for sale, and God willing, it will never be for sale."

Cari tried to keep from squirming in her chair. She felt like she was eavesdropping on a private conversation. She chewed on the inside of her cheek as the conversation continued around her. Lydia sure was getting attacked from every side. The break-ins, the realtor, the property taxes, and now issues with her mortgage were all threatening the business she grew up loving. She remembered Genevieve thinking everything was related. She needed to do some research to prove it.

She sat up in her chair and cleared her throat. "Uh, sorry to interrupt. Can I get the name and address you got from Deputy Yarrow? I can run some searches and maybe figure out who this guy is."

Jack ran a hand over his short hair and started shuffling items around on the desk. "We only got an address, not a name. We wrote it down here somewhere. Just a sec."

Lydia put a hand on Jack's arm to stop him from making a bigger mess of the papers on the desk. She pulled out the top drawer and removed a yellow sticky note. "Jack, it's right here. I put it in the top drawer so it wouldn't get lost in all the paperwork."

"And this is why you're better at running this business than I would ever be," Jack told her.

Cari pulled out her phone. "Can I just snap a quick photo of that?"

Lydia handed it to Cari and she used her phone camera to get an image of the note.

Bob stood up. "Why don't we get out of your hair while you talk through the mortgage stuff? We'll keep you updated."

Cari pushed back from the desk and followed Bob out of the office. She was glad her head didn't hurt anymore. Vacation or not, it was time to track down this intruder.

Chapter 12

As Cari followed Bob up the stairs back to their room, her cell phone buzzed with an incoming call. She checked her watch and stopped climbing the stairs when she saw it was Grandmother calling. She usually called her grandmother, not the other way around.

"Hey, Grandmother! Is everything okay?"

Her grandmother didn't immediately respond. "Grandmother? Are you there?"

Grandmother chuckled. "Sorry, dear. I had the phone on mute somehow. Old people and technology, we just don't mix."

"I think you do great with tech, Grandmother." Cari admonished her.

"I'm sorry to bother you on your trip, but your concussion has me a little worried," she admitted.

"I'm doing much better already, I promise. I don't even have a headache anymore."

She heard her grandmother exhale. "That is such a relief to hear...well, I got your sister packed up and out the door this morning. She and the kids have plans to meet Robby at the lake this afternoon. I hope it's, um, well, it will be a fun little excursion for them."

Cari furrowed her brow. "Yeah, the lake is always fun, right?"

"Of course, dear. By the way, did the police catch the intruder yet? I'm sure Bob's aunt is ready to move past all that."

"They're making progress. Actually, I'm trying to help. The suspect seems to have multiple identities and several false addresses. I offered to do some research to see if I could help track him down."

"*Just* research? You're not out there chasing after criminals with a concussion, right?"

Cari smiled at her grandmother's concern. "Yes, Grandmother, just research. Bob's aunt has a lot going on right now and I want to help any way I can."

"Well, be safe. I can't imagine you'll be in any danger on your computer, but I also never expected you to get a concussion from a leisurely kayaking excursion. Take care of yourself, sweetheart."

"I will, Grandmother. I love you."

"I love you more."

Cari put her phone back into her pocket and looked up at Bob. He was reading something on his phone. He caught her staring at him and quickly shoved the phone into his pocket.

"Everything okay?" he asked her.

"Just Grandmother being worried about me," Cari frowned remembering what her grandmother said.

"What?" Bob asked with concern.

"She made a funny comment the other day, but I'd forgotten about it. Something is bothering her about my sister. I'll have to try and remember to ask her about it the next time we chat," Cari said slowly.

Bob nodded. "Hopefully, it's nothing major."

They continued up the stairs and unlocked their room. Cari immediately got out her laptop and put it on the coffee table.

"Hey, before I start looking for this guy, you need to finish telling me your grandfather's tall tale," Cari encouraged him.

"Oh, right. I'd almost forgotten all about that. Where was I?"

"He had just decided to double-cross his friends and take all the gold back to Pennsylvania with him," Cari prodded him.

"That's right. Let me think..." he paused and clicked his tongue. "When it was his turn to keep watch one night, he gathered up the gold they'd mined and left their campsite while it was still dark. He had a horse, which he led out of camp on foot to keep from waking his friends."

"Well, I doubt they were his friends at this point," Cari remarked.

"True. The man knew it wouldn't be long before his *friends* caught up with him, so rather than get caught with the gold in his saddlebags, he 'borrowed' a rowboat and went out to one of the caves along Lake Superior. Using his pick axe, he dug into the wall of the cave and hid the bag of gold. He planned to return a few weeks later to recover it. He figured his friends would eventually give up and move on, so he drew a map of the area."

"But his friends could just as easily take the map from him!" Cari interjected.

"Yes, and he realized that, which is why he returned to the boarding house. He asked permission to hide the map within the house, but wouldn't say where. He promised to return once the dust settled and retrieve the map. Willoughby didn't want any trouble but felt bad for the young man. He offered to hide his horse at a nearby farm and suggested the man continue his journey in the rowboat."

"That's like aiding and abetting! He must have really had a soft spot for romance."

"Nobody's perfect," Bob joked.

Cari looked at her watch and chewed on the inside of her cheek. "Ugh, I *really* want to hear how the story ends, but I also want to figure out who this guy is."

"I've heard the story so many times. Don't worry. I won't forget it. Let's do some sleuthing."

"Okay, we have two names and three addresses for this guy," she said to Bob.

"It's possible none of those are his real name. I mean, none of the addresses are his actual home address."

"That's true. I wonder what would happen if I looked up the dry cleaner's phone number and asked for Jasper Benavidez."

"Is that the third address? I didn't look at the sticky note."

Cari nodded. "Yeah, that's it."

"I wouldn't call. It's possible the dry-cleaning place doesn't even know he put their address down, but it's also possible he works there or someone there knows him and if you call, it could make him go deeper into hiding."

"For burglary?"

"I mean, he's clearly putting effort into covering his tracks," Bob reminded her.

"True. Honestly, it really feels like there's more going on here," Cari told him. "Let me pull up this dry-cleaning business and see what I can find."

She logged into her computer and opened the web browser. She navigated to the LexisNexis website and started to enter her login information. She had never used the database for personal inquiries, only things related to her job as a journalist. She wondered if Ollaman would be upset if he learned what she was up to. The *Beagle* paid for her subscription. *What was the motto? Ask forgiveness, not permission!* She clicked enter and logged into her account.

It took her a few tries to find the correct business. The address Lydia gave her was in Duluth, Minnesota and the business was part of a chain, though it seemed like they operated it as a franchise. Once she found the one with the matching address, she started to reach for her messenger bag to get a notebook out. Then she remembered she'd emptied the bag of most of its contents for the trip.

"Hey, Bob?"

He looked up from his phone and mumbled something unintelligible.

"Do you have any paper and something to write with? I want to take a few notes."

"Paper? Uh, I can get some from Aunt Lydia. I'll be right back."

While she waited, she scrolled through the information related to the business. It was owned by someone named Ricki Plenip and had a long list of employees. Financially, the place seemed fine, though she had to admit she didn't know the first thing about a dry-cleaning business. They had a consistent income, no large debts, and not a lot of employee turnover.

She scrolled through the list of employees, but none of them were named Jasper Benavidez or Lucien Merrick. Cari drummed her fingers on the table. The business had to have a connection to the intruder. He couldn't just pick a random address and hope no one would realize it wasn't his. *And why does a petty thief have multiple aliases?* She decided to give Genevieve a call. Maybe talking through the case would give her a better perspective. She got out her phone and called her friend.

"Hey, Cari. Track down the intruder, yet?"

"No, that's why I'm calling. The guy has multiple addresses—at least three that the police have found. None of them are valid residential addresses. The most recent one is a dry-cleaning business. I looked it up on LexisNexis, but everything looks normal. None of the names on the employee list match any of the aliases. We really don't know if we have the guy's real name yet."

"Hmmm…it feels overly complex for someone who is *just* breaking into a B&B."

Cari put her hand palm up in agreement. "I think so too, but I can't figure out why."

"Tell me everything again. The break-ins, what's been taken, anything else that's giving Bob's aunt trouble with the business. This person has some sort of end goal. He's not just a teenager with too much time on his hands."

"Let's see. I think the break-ins started about a month ago. I don't have the exact dates or anything. They broke a window on the ground floor twice, I think. Then used a crow bar or something to get into the basement. That's when he stole a guestbook—"

"So you're sure now that it *was* stolen? Why steal a guestbook?" Genevieve interrupted.

Cari laughed. "I know, apparently it was the oldest one, but it's not like it's a collector's item or something. It's completely worthless, monetarily speaking, but it's definitely gone."

"Random. Okay. Keep going."

"And then there's the most recent time when he broke into our guest room. They found palm prints on the basement door and the balcony railing that match someone named Lucien Merrick. It turns out Lucien is an alias for Jasper Benavidez or maybe it's the other way around. Anyway, Lucien, posing as Jasper, stayed at the B&B and helped Lydia clean up the broken glass from the second break-in."

"But he actually broke the glass himself?"

"Allegedly," Cari corrected her.

"Right. Now you have a third address, which happens to be a dry-cleaning business. Hmmm…I think you should go through social media posts and see if any of the employees have a connection to your guy Lucien/Jasper/whatever."

"That's a good idea," Cari responded. "I'll make a note…rats. I sent Bob downstairs for paper and a pen. He should have been back by now."

"Maybe he's visiting with his aunt," Genevieve suggested.

"Or his parents…" Cari said absentmindedly.

"Wait, what?" Genevieve almost shouted into the phone.

Cari pulled the phone away from her ear in response. "Oh, I didn't tell you. His parents came to town the other day too."

"As a surprise, or?" Geneveive asked.

"No, I mean, I was surprised, but Lydia needs to get a security system and she's also getting harassed by a realtor who claims to have a buyer interested in her business—"

"Hold up. Someone is trying to buy the bed and breakfast?"

Cari could hear the curiosity in her friend's voice. "It's not even for sale. He keeps calling and even had someone drop an offer by her office the other day. Bob's dad is an accountant, so he offered to help manage some of these things while she works with the sheriff's department on the break-ins."

"But think about it. That could be the guy's end game. He wants the business. He's trying to knock down the price by *staging* burglaries, which will scare off potential guests and make her lose money, which makes her more likely to agree to selling."

"But if he drives the business into the ground, what does he gain?"

"He could put any business there. It sounds like it's prime real estate with its adjacency to the lake and everything."

Cari chewed the inside of her cheek before responding. "I don't know. Part of the appeal of this place is how it's been in the same family for over a century. You lose that when the property changes hands."

Genevieve clicked her tongue. "Well, that's my take on it. Look for overlap with that realtor or see if you can figure out who the client is."

"I'll put it on the list, if Bob ever gets back here with some paper," she laughed.

"Keep me posted. How is your head, by the way?"

"I'm definitely on the mend. I'll be good as new in no time," she reassured her friend.

157

"Tell Bob hi for me. And get back to running. No vacation from training!" Genevieve laughed.

"Yeah, I'll be sure to bring that up," Cari said just as Bob opened the door.

"Bring what up?" Bob asked with his eyebrows raised.

"The 5k!" Genevieve shouted into the phone, making Cari flinch.

"Oh, right. Yeah, logging all sorts of miles out here. The most ever," he laughed.

"I'll talk to you later, Cari. Take care of yourself."

"You too. Bye!" Cari said and ended the call.

Bob extended his hand with a pad of paper and a ball point pen. "Your writing materials, m'lady."

Cari laughed. "Thank you, kind sir."

"By the way, it's already 4:30..." he said somewhat cautiously.

She blinked, unsure why he was telling her the time.

"Cocktail hour?" he reminded her.

Cari exhaled. "Right. Let me make two notes so I don't forget. I probably need to work a little magic with my makeup again so your mom doesn't think you're dating a troll."

"She would never think that," Bob responded.

"I mean, have you seen my face today?"

Bob pressed his lips together before speaking. "I mean—"

"Don't even try to lie! It's okay. I'm getting used to my new look. The bruises will fade away eventually. My days as a troll are numbered."

She jotted down Genevieve's two ideas and then closed her laptop. Time to impress the parents.

* * * * *

Cari inspected herself in the mirror one more time. She scrunched her curls and tried to keep from tucking them behind her ears. She had to get creative to cover as much of her bruised face as she could. Bob had told her the restaurant tonight was "dressy casual", which was meaningless, but she opted for a sundress and her strappy sandals. It would be another short walk after the cocktail hour with his parents. She bit her lip and looked herself over again.

"Almost ready?" Bob called out from the bedroom.

Cari sighed. "As ready as I can be."

She turned off the bathroom light and stepped into the room where Bob was standing, looking at his watch. "How do I look?"

"Fantastic," he smiled when he looked up and took her into his arms.

"Any topics I should avoid over cocktails?" she asked nervously.

"Uh, I can't think of any. My parents are pretty calm overall. You'll like them…and they will love you. Don't worry."

"Easier said than done," she forced a smile. "I don't want to be late, so let's head on downstairs."

"After you," he said, opening the door for her.

"Thank you," she pecked him on the cheek on her way by, making him blush.

When they reached the bottom of the stairs, Bob grabbed her hand in his. She slowly exhaled and walked alongside him. She wasn't sure where they were meeting his parents.

"Do we go to the dining room for cocktail hour?"

"My parents wanted to meet outside. Is that okay? It doesn't look too windy out."

"It will be great," she squeezed his hand with more confidence than she felt.

Bob led her outside. Jack and Margie were already seated at one of the porch tables. Cari wasn't sure if it was really part of the business' dining area or a perk of being related to the owner. She decided not to ask. When his parents saw them approaching, they both stood up from the table.

"Hello! Thanks so much for joining us for our little cocktail hour. Have a seat. The waiter should be back out any moment," Margie said with a big smile and handed Cari a small beverage menu.

Cari returned the smile and took the menu from her. She sat next to Jack while Bob took a seat by his mom. She stifled a laugh after looking at Jack and Bob in close proximity. They were both wearing a light blue polo shirt and khaki pants with tan loafers. If Bob ever wondered what he'd look like in the future, he needed only to look at his father. A voice pulled Cari from her thoughts.

"Oh goodness!" Lydia exclaimed while placing two drinks in front of Margie and Jack. "What am I going to do with the two of you? You're dressed exactly the same. It's like you're wearing a uniform."

Jack's face registered alarm. "Oh rats. We should have picked a different day," his eyes sparkled with a hint of mischief. "I only wear this on days that end in Y."

Bob groaned and dragged a hand over his face. "Dad, that joke stopped being funny literally decades ago."

"That's too bad. It's one of my best jokes."

Lydia rolled her eyes and then turned to Bob and Cari. "Let me grab your drink orders and I'll have them right out."

Cari scanned the menu. "I'll get a Superior Mojito, please."

"And I'll have an Old Fashioned. Thanks, Aunt Lydia."

"These are on the house," she put her hand up when Jack started to object. "No. I insist. It's my treat. I'll have those out in a jiffy."

Margie squeezed her sister-in-law's arm before she walked away. "Cari, how are you feeling? It sounded like quite the accident."

"It definitely caught me off guard. Thank you for asking; my headache seems to be gone finally," she knocked on the table jokingly. "Now, if I could get rid of these bruises, it would really be nice."

"You can hardly tell at all," Margie told her.

Cari smiled. "You're too kind. I've sworn off all selfies for the time being. I had to really work some magic with my makeup and I still look a bit like an abused troll."

Margie shook her head in disagreement. "You're gorgeous, with or without bruises. Now, tell me about yourself. Bob has told us you're a journalist. It sounds like you're also quite the amateur sleuth."

Cari felt herself blush. "I don't know if I'd call myself a sleuth, but I do like to put a good story together. Sometimes that means finding the bad guy's secrets."

"But you've gained the trust of your local police department, right? That seems very remarkable. I always thought the police steered clear of the media whenever possible, but maybe that's not reality except in the crime novels I read."

Cari chuckled. "It did take a little persuasion to get on the good side of the police department. My predecessor was a little less amiable with most law enforcement. I've had to rebuild some bridges, but things seem to be on track for now."

Lydia set their drinks on the table and slipped back inside. They each raised their glasses toward the middle of the table.

"To health and healing," Margie said as she clinked her glass against the others.

Cari took a sip of her drink before setting it back on the table. It was a very good mojito.

Jack spoke up. "Well, I'm impressed with your writing and your sleuthing. I've never been very good with the written word. I'm more of a numbers guy."

She grinned at him. "We all have our strengths, right? That's what my grandmother always says."

161

Margie laughed. "She's right. Say, your locket is lovely. Is it a family heirloom?"

Cari clasped the charm in her hand. "Thank you. No, it's always just been mine. My grandmother gave it to me when I graduated from high school." She opened the locket to show them the picture.

"What a sweet picture. The two of you must be very close."

Cari beamed. "We are. She is...as they say on Grey's Anatomy, 'my person'."

"Not to change the subject, but has Bob told you about the legend of The Boarding House?" Jack asked with a gleam in his eye.

Cari furrowed her eyebrows trying to figure out what he meant when it hit her: the folk story! "Oh, he started telling it but hasn't finished yet."

Bob turned red. "I mean, I basically finished."

"Where did he stop, my dear?" Jack asked Cari.

"Let's see. I think the young man was getting ready to leave by boat while Grandfather Willoughby hid his horse at a nearby farm or something."

"Bob," Jack scolded. "You aren't even close to being finished."

Bob rolled his eyes in response.

"Okay, I can tell it better anyway. When Willoughby returned from hiding the horse, the young man was nowhere to be found. He assumed he'd done what he came to do and was already on his way back to the lake. However, several days later, they received word of a body washing up on the shore of what became known as Specter Island."

"That's so far away. Surely, it couldn't have been—"

"But it was. The young man had been badly beaten and drowned in the lake. Willoughby was the one who identified the body. The authorities at the time had no idea what had happened. Not wanting to bring trouble to his house and business,

162

Willoughby kept quiet about seeing the man twice. He only mentioned his traveling through with friends nearly a month before."

"Wait, you said 'what became known as Specter Island.' Was the island unnamed before?" Cari questioned him.

"Well, here's where some of the folklore comes in—"

"Oh, I think I've already heard a bit of folklore already," Cari laughed.

Jack grinned mischievously. "In the days and weeks that followed, locals reported sightings of a ghost haunting the shorelines and caves of Lake Superior. They decided it was the ghost of the young man protecting his treasure and named the island where he died 'Specter Island'."

"Wait, spector? Is that spelled with an o, like *inspector*?" Cari asked him.

"No, it's spelled S-P-E-C-T-E-R. It means spirit or ghost or phantom."

"How ominous. But wait. What about the four friends? Didn't they keep looking for the treasure? Didn't someone find the horse?"

Bob laughed. "We said it was folklore, not a true story. Every year, when my grandfather told this story, all of us kids wanted to tear the Boarding House apart and look for the map. We wanted to search for the treasure and be rich!"

Cari giggled. "I bet your grandfather loved telling that story to you…"

"Right up until the point we begged to peel the wallpaper off the walls and dig up the garden," Bob admitted.

"Surely this story got around though. Children love a good treasure hunt story. How was this place not teeming with treasure hunters?"

Bob laughed. "None of the adults believed the veracity of the story and most of the children lived out of town. Even if we shared it with our classmates back home, it was still just a tall tale. I doubt many people outside of my family have heard it."

"It's news to me," Cari laughed with him.

Margie nodded in understanding. "Now it's my turn to change the subject. Bob mentioned you volunteer together at a local shelter. What sort of work do you do there?"

"Well, my handiness is limited, so they've relegated me to flipping pancakes. I even had to get a little instruction from one of the people in line on how to do that. Bob is usually given an outdoor assignment, like building garden beds or other improvements to the facility. I am a terrible gardener, so I don't think they'll ever ask me to help out there."

"Do you go once a month? I can't remember what Bob told us," Margie admitted.

"We initially signed up to go once a month, but it was such a good experience that we signed up to be weekly volunteers. They have substitutes they can call on if someone is sick or out of town, like we are now. It's a really great place. I think it helps a lot of people."

"That's wonderful. Bob claims you've talked him into running a 5k next month. Some kind of contest?" Margie asked her.

"Oh, yes! It came about as a dare, I guess. One of the other CSU guys and my friend Genevieve—uh, she's a detective in Brenington...anyway, we're all doing it together. Our training has gotten a bit derailed out here though."

Jack's jaw dropped. "You aren't trying to run out here, are you? It's like one big hill. Did you run up these hills, Bob?"

Bob took the final drink from his cocktail and shifted uncomfortably in his seat. "No. And since the kayaking accident, no one has done any running, which is just fine with me." He paused while they laughed. "Well, speaking of running. I hate to drink and run, but we need to get to our reservation."

Cari finished her own drink and pushed back from the table. "It was nice to chat with you. I'm glad you invited us to do this."

"Me too. Enjoy your dinner," Margie told her.

Bob stood up and turned to his dad. "Did Aunt Lydia show you the offer from the realtor? I still think it's odd someone would try to buy a place that isn't for sale."

"I mean, it never hurts to ask, right?" Jack asked. "I did look at it. It was horribly low. It's almost like it was a joke. I told her to ignore it."

Bob nodded slowly in response. "That's very strange. I don't understand real estate people at all. Well, we'll be seeing you around, I'm sure."

He shook his parents' hands and then motioned for Cari to lead the way. They walked down the porch steps to the sidewalk. Cari couldn't remember the name of the place they were going for dinner, but figured it was within walking distance like the other place had been.

"I hope you didn't feel like you were under the microscope there," Bob told her after they had walked for a block.

"What? Not at all! Your parents are nice. I wish I could have asked them about themselves though. I feel like I talked the whole time. I barely finished my cocktail."

He squeezed her hand. "I'm glad you liked them."

"I know you told me where we're eating tonight, but my brain has forgotten. It's still a little tired, I guess," Cari said sheepishly.

He pointed ahead at a building shaped like a lighthouse. "The Lighthouse Restaurant. It has two floors, and I got us a table on the top floor. I'm glad you're feeling like eating out tonight. It's fun to see the lake from up higher."

Bob's phone buzzed with a text right as they reached the door to the restaurant. He quickly checked it and then returned it to his pocket without saying anything. Cari tried not to overthink why he continued to be so secretive with his phone. Nonetheless, her mind settled on the mystery surrounding his childhood friend Contessa. Cari hated feeling jealous, especially when she wasn't even sure if she needed to be.

Chapter 13

Cari ran along the beach; the wind was blowing her hair into her face. She swiped at it and looked over her shoulder. The man was still coming after her and seemed to be gaining on her. She stepped on a piece of driftwood and yelped in pain. Where were her shoes? She willed herself to keep going. "Cariiii…" the man called out to her in a haunting voice. "Cariiii…"

"Cari!" Bob gently shook her awake.

"Huh?" She blinked her eyes and realized she was in their suite in the bed and breakfast.

"You were having some kind of nightmare. It looked like you were running, which I can understand. Running is a bit of a nightmare."

She gave him a playful punch in the shoulder. "I was on the beach without shoes and this man was chasing me."

"Maybe it was the ghost of Specter Island! He came to haunt your dreams," Bob laughed.

She rolled her eyes. "Very funny. I was really scared."

Wrapping his arms around her he said, "Well, I'm glad the ghost didn't capture you. How are you feeling today? I have a lighthouse tour booked."

Cari tilted her head in thought. "Do we have to kayak?"

Bob grinned, "No, but we do take a ferry. Are you okay with going back on the lake?"

Cari gave him a pointed look. "When have you ever known me to shy away from something?"

He furrowed his brow. "Well, if it involves cleaning..."

"Shut it. I'm in for the lighthouse tour. What time does it start?"

"We don't need to get to the ferry until ten o'clock. Thankfully, you woke both of us up in plenty of time, so we can have a leisurely morning."

She looked at her watch. It wasn't even seven a.m. yet. "Sorry about that. I call dibs on the first shower!"

She jumped out of bed and left Bob with his jaw hanging open. She looked in the mirror before turning on the water and gave herself a nod. The bruises had faded quite a bit since the day before.

Once the water was warm, she stepped under the nozzle and thought about her conversation with Genevieve from the day before. Her friend thought everything was connected. Usually, Cari was the one trying to convince everyone else about a big conspiracy. She still couldn't understand why someone would want the bed and breakfast so badly. Did they just want the space for a different business? She shook her head in confusion. There was more to this situation.

Wanting to dig into the dry-cleaning business a bit more, she quickly finished showering and wrapped a towel around herself. Bob was on his phone when she entered the room and didn't initially notice her. She cleared her throat.

"The bathroom's all yours now."

His head snapped up. "Oh! You startled me. I'll be quick and we can go down to breakfast."

"Take your time. I'm going to do a little more research into the dry-cleaning business. Maybe I'll find some sort of connection to our mystery man."

"I would say the sheriff's department has it under control, but I know that won't stop you. So, happy sleuthing."

He shut the bathroom door and Cari pulled out some casual clothes for the day of sightseeing. She figured they would be doing some walking, so she tugged on her sneakers instead of her sandals. Her laptop was still on the coffee table where she left it the previous afternoon. She turned it back on and logged in. LexisNexis had a message on the screen telling her that her session had timed out. She re-entered her login information and found the dry-cleaning business again.

The business was owned by an LLC, a limited liability company, which she knew had something to do with how the business was taxed. She jotted it down on the notepad so she could read more about it later. She wondered if the police found any connections between the intruder and the dry-cleaning business yet. She drummed her fingers on the table.

Alex had done her a favor by giving her the sheriff's personal contact information. She knew if she called the station, they might not give her any information as it was an open investigation. If she called the sheriff's cell phone, though...would she answer? And would she be annoyed with Cari for calling?

Cari unplugged her phone from the charger and unlocked it. She scrolled through her contacts list and hovered her thumb over the phone symbol next to the name Janice Maruthers. Her knee was bouncing with nervous energy as she mentally debated making the call. She started to lower her thumb, when an incoming call flashed on the screen.

"Hi, Grandmother! You probably just stopped me from doing something I shouldn't."

"Oh? And what is that?"

"Well, Alex—Genevieve's partner—"

"Yes, I know who Alex is," her grandmother assured her.

"Alex gave me the personal cell phone number for the county sheriff. I was thinking about calling her to get an update on the case and maybe talk through some ideas Genevieve had…" she trailed off.

"But you realized you have no justifiable reason to get those results and you'd be abusing your association with Alex if you called?"

Cari blushed. "It crossed my mind, but I hadn't convinced myself not to do it."

"Well, I'm glad I called when I did."

"Usually, I'm the one calling you. You're wise, but I know you didn't know what I was up to. Why did you really call?"

"Well," her grandmother drew the word out. "Maybe I should, what is it the kids say? Stay in my lane? I've been worrying about your sister…and Robby. She admitted she's having second thoughts about the job he took in New York."

"Does she miss Florida?"

"Oh, no. Nothing like that. She loves being back in New York. It's the job itself. She said Robby is working weird hours. He sometimes takes phone calls in the garage. If she asks him about it, he gets agitated…" Grandmother trailed off.

"That does sound troubling. What's she going to do?"

"She doesn't know. If he won't talk about it, there isn't a lot she can do. Maybe he'll open up about it soon." She took a quick breath and released it. "You sound somewhat less tired. How are you doing?"

"I woke up without a headache today, so that is an improvement," she began.

"But…" her grandmother encouraged.

"But I also had a nightmare where I was being chased by a man or a ghost or something down the beach here. It was terrifying."

"Oh dear! What would have triggered a dream like that?"

"Well, Bob and his dad told me this tall tale, folklore really, the other day. It ended with something about a ghost haunting the island to protect his treasure."

"Sounds very ominous. Have you been looking for the ghost's treasure?"

Cari laughed. "What? No! There is no treasure. It's just a spooky story his grandfather used to tell the kids when the family was all gathered here."

"Is it a local legend?"

"The ghost?" Cari asked with confusion.

"The story. Is it something everyone knows?"

"Oh, hmmm. That's a good question," Cari tried to recall Bob's explanation. "I don't think it's a local legend. He said it was a story his grandpa shared, but it wasn't something the community was familiar with. I wonder…"

"What?"

"Well, part of the story claims the island off the coast here—it's called 'Specter Island'—was so named because of the ghost haunting the island, but I thought that was silly. The story, as his grandfather told it, began in like 1849. I think the island would have been named long before then."

"That makes sense," Grandmother agreed.

"I wonder if someone else has heard the story. Maybe that's what this is all about. Someone else must know this story. Thank you, Grandmother! I've gotta go. I love you.'"

"I love you more."

Cari ended the call and the screen returned to the sheriff's contact info. Cari backed out of it and set her phone aside. She opened a new tab, which opened an internet search engine. She typed in 'how was Specter Island named" and hit enter. Several results popped up. She skimmed the summaries of the first few. They were all historical websites and none of them said anything about a ghost. She scrolled through the list, looking for the word

171

ghost or haunted, but none of them mentioned anything of the sort. She added "ghost" to the search and hit enter. It gave her zero results. She sighed. Maybe Genevieve's theory was right. Maybe—

"You look deep in thought..." Bob started to say, making Cari jump.

She laughed. "I was down the rabbit hole, chasing a theory."

"Did you find it?"

She shook her head. "I'm not sure. I think I ended up where I started. Are you sure no one else knows your family's *legend of The Boarding House* story?"

"It's not like it's published anywhere, why?"

"What if this guy is breaking in to try to find the treasure map?"

Bob snorted. "That's crazy. Who would actually believe that story was true?"

"I don't know. I can't seem to shake any sense into this investigation at all."

"Maybe eating breakfast will help. I'm pretty hungry."

"Might as well. Maybe a change of scenery will give me a fresh idea."

* * * * *

Lydia sat on the porch and watched her guests enjoying breakfast. She was on her third cup of coffee already. Jack had talked her into calling the bank about refinancing her mortgage. She had been up half the night worrying about all the different ways they might say no.

She smoothed out her apron and tried to relax. She hadn't been late on a single payment and her credit should be decent. She didn't have any outstanding debts to the oncologist's office anymore either. The Boarding House's financial outlook wasn't so rosy. Without looking at the books, she couldn't say with confidence that they'd actually been in the black for the past month. Not to mention the additional cost of the security system being installed today; she knew that would tilt the scale further into the red.

Lydia let out a sigh and got up from the table. Bob and Cari had just been seated in the dining room. She wondered what adventure Bob had planned for them today or if Cari still needed to take it easy because of her concussion. She squinted as she peered through the glass.

"And who are you spying on?"

Lydia nearly dropped her coffee mug. "Jack! You rascal. You almost made me break something."

"Oh, it's our two lovebirds. You're as bad as Margie. She tried to get me to ask the people at the table next to theirs to move, so we could sit closer to them. Don't worry," he said to Lydia's open mouth. "I told her I would do nothing of the sort. This was *after* I had to get onto her again for texting Bob nonstop about when he's going to propose."

"Oh my gracious…poor Bob. I didn't see Margie enter the dining room. Where is she?"

"She realized she left her phone in the room and went back to grab it. She'll be down in a minute," he paused. "Are you ready for the security installation today?"

She nodded slowly. "As ready as I can be. I hope it isn't too disruptive to the guests."

"I think they will be happy to see the upgrade."

"About the bank…" Lydia tried to come up with the right words.

"Hey, I told you. Margie and I will co-sign if it will get you a better rate. We can put down some principle too—"

Lydia put up her hands in protest. "Jack, no. You don't need to do that."

"Lydia, you have been through the gauntlet lately. This isn't just your business, it's your home. Let me help carry your burden."

"I will repay every penny."

"It isn't necessary. And, we don't know what the bank is going to say. You can't usually refinance in one visit. They need lots of paperwork. We can get the ball rolling on it. I know we can get you a better rate than the one you have." Jack reassured her.

"There's Margie now. Why don't you join her for breakfast? I'm going to make my rounds through the building and see if anyone needs my assistance."

"Okay, but we're going to the bank at nine."

"You made an appointment?" Lydia asked, shocked.

"No, that's what time it opens. I don't want to have to wait in line to see one of the bankers."

"But the security guys are arriving at ten," she protested.

"And Margie can help them get started if we aren't back yet. No more excuses."

She pointed a finger at him. "You sure are bossy for being a little brother."

"I've been told it's one of my strongest qualities," he joked.

"It's not a compliment!" she laughed, unable to put any sternness in her voice.

* * * * *

Bob slipped his hand into his pocket and felt the ring box. For once, he was thankful Cari and Genevieve had made him start running. His pants and shorts were a bit baggy on him now and made hiding the ring in his pocket less noticeable. He had feigned forgetting something in the room so he could call ahead to the large lighthouse on Specter Island. He wanted to make sure they could still climb the winding staircase to the top. The waitress at breakfast had mentioned disappointment over many of the lighthouses refusing access to tourists over the last few years. He looked up the number and dialed it.

"Specter Island Lighthouse, this is Sherry. How can I help you?"

"Hi, this is Bob Hursley. I'll be visiting the lighthouse with my, uh, girlfriend later today...as part of the ferry tour..." he stuttered.

"Yes?" Sherry asked with a bit of impatience.

"Sorry, um, do you still allow the visitors on the ferry tour to take the stairs up to the top?"

"No, sir. I'm sorry. The stairs are being repaired right now. Ever since the state installed more modern things like radar beacons and lighted navigational aids, the lighthouses stopped being maintained regularly. The lighthouse isn't manned anymore; it's controlled electronically. You can still tour the grounds surrounding our lighthouse, though."

Bob's shoulders sagged. So much for the romantic proposal at the top of the tallest lighthouse in Wisconsin. "I understand. Thank you."

He picked his backpack up from the floor and swung it onto one shoulder. He was running out of time to propose if he wanted to do it while they were on vacation together. He needed to come up with a new plan. He opened the door and locked it behind him. Cari was waiting in the lobby when he made it to the base of the stairs. She smiled at him, but tilted her head with curiosity. He realized she was wondering what it was he'd forgotten in the room and had no idea what he'd tell her. He decided to pretend like he hadn't noticed she looked curious.

"Ready to drive over to the ferry?" he asked.

"I am. Your mom asked me to remind you to take photos for her. She said something about replacing the set in the sitting room?" Cari asked in confusion.

Bob snorted. "She knows I take terrible photos. She has a whole display of my disastrous attempts at being picturesque. Several of the photos have portions of my thumb or finger in them."

Cari laughed loudly, making some guests turn their heads from the dining room. "Oh my goodness. That is fantastic. I can't believe she did that. Your mom is *funny*."

Bob blushed. "Maybe we can get her a few improvements for her collection."

* * * * *

Lydia tried to keep from trudging up the steps to The Boarding House. The meeting with the banker hadn't been *that* bad, but it was just more work on top of all the work she already needed to do. She didn't want Jack to think she was ungrateful for his help, but she wasn't looking forward to gathering all the documents the banker requested either.

"Cheer up, Lyd. We can get these docs together in no time." Jack said. Apparently, he was a mind reader now too.

She sighed. "I know. I wish it was easier to get everything straightened out. I feel like I've made a mess of literally everything."

Jack squeezed her shoulder and started to speak when her cell phone rang. It was someone from the sheriff's office.

"This is Lydia Fairchild."

"Lydia, I'm glad I caught you. I have an update on your case," Deputy Yarrow told her.

Lydia bit her lip. She didn't want to get her hopes up. "Yes?"

"Well, we looked into the dry-cleaning business…the newest address we found for the intruder. It's owned by a Ricki Plenip, but we couldn't find anything or anyone that connects her to any of the names we have for the intruder."

Lydia exhaled. "What about employees? Maybe one of them?"

"Yes, we are looking at everyone on the list, but so far, we haven't found a connection."

Lydia's shoulders drooped down. "Well, I appreciate the update."

"We're not giving up, Lydia. I'll be in touch." He ended the call.

Jack looked at her with his eyebrows raised. "Sheriff Maruthers?"

Lydia shook her head no. "No, it was her deputy, Yarrow."

"I take it he didn't have good news for you."

"No, I mean, I guess it wasn't necessarily bad news. They just can't find the man. He's like an enigma!" She threw her hands up in the air in frustration.

"He can't hide forever, especially if there's something here he's really looking for. He'll come looking again. And, with the new security system, you'll know when he gets here."

"I've known when he was here before! I was with him *right after* the second break-in and he played me for a fool, which apparently, I am." Lydia raised her voice.

Jack put his hands up and lowered them down slowly. "Whoa. You are not a fool. This guy is smart. He has a plan and he's executing it extremely well. That doesn't mean he's infallible. Let's go inside. We don't need to argue on the porch in front of God and everyone."

Lydia looked around and saw a couple of people in grey polos staring at her. She had forgotten the security company was starting the installation at ten. She grimaced and then tried to paste on a reassuring smile before following Jack inside. Margie was waving at them to join her in the office.

"Thanks for holding down the fort, Margie. I really appreciate it," Lydia said as she entered the office.

"Well, don't thank me yet. A reporter from the local newspaper has called here for you twice in the last half hour. He wouldn't tell me why, but he left his number the second time." She handed her a sticky note.

Lydia took the note and read the information off of it. "Do you think it's about the break-ins? It's not like I've kept it under wraps, but I didn't really want it plastered all over the news. It feels like we're so close to putting a stop to it too."

She walked around her desk and sat down in the chair. She really didn't want to call the reporter back, but she was afraid of what he might print if she didn't speak with him. She grabbed the phone receiver and dialed his number.

"Harborville Gazette. This is Smitty. How can I help you today?"

"Hi, uh, Mr. uh, Smitty. This is Lydia Fairchild. I had a message to call you." Lydia stammered.

"Ah, yes, Ms. Fairchild. Can I call you Lydia? Lydia, my dear. I'm finishing up a story about the recent break-ins The Boarding House has experienced. I was hoping to get a comment from you. What are you doing to stop them? My source says they started almost a month ago."

Lydia gulped and felt the color draining from her face. "We're, um, we hired, um, the sheriff…"

Margie grabbed the phone from Lydia. "Hi again, Smitty, is it?"

"Who's this?"

"This is Lydia's receptionist. She would like to make a statement regarding the break-ins, but needs some time to get it together. She's working with the sheriff's department and needs to review her comments with them before they can be formally printed. Can you give us a day or two?"

"No can do. This story is set to go live at six o'clock tonight. I'll need the statement by three so the formatters can do their thing prior to posting. Our sources tell us there have been four break-ins already and business has dropped considerably. Is Ms. Fairchild in danger of closing?"

"Three p.m., Smitty. We'll be in touch." Margie hung up the phone.

"This cannot be happening. Why is he doing this? Why wouldn't he want to be supportive of a local business? I'm not trying to sweep this under the rug. I've informed all current and future guests about the break-ins. Posting this on the internet could ruin me. No one will stay here if it sounds unsafe." Lydia's eyes filled with tears.

Margie gripped her shoulder. "Take a deep breath. We have our own specialist for this guy Smitty. Cari is a journalist. She'll know just how to word your statement that will paint everything in the best light."

"Do you really think we need to ask the Sheriff before we give this guy a statement?" Lydia asked her.

"I don't think we need to give them every detail. Cari will know what to do. Bob says she is *very* good at her job. I'll text him now."

* * * * *

Cari gazed into the distance as the ferry continued across the lake. The first two lighthouses were on two of the twelve Apostle Islands which were scattered between the mainland and the larger Specter Island. The tour guide told them the lighthouses were two of the smaller ones on the lake. He liked stopping at them because they still allowed tourists to climb to the top and look out the window.

It took about ten minutes for the ferry to reach each stop and then another five or ten for everyone to climb ashore. Even though Bob had promised his mom he would take photos, he hadn't gotten his phone out once since they stepped foot on the ferry. Cari heard it buzz a few times, but it seemed like he was set on ignoring whoever was trying to communicate with him. She reached for his hand, but he slipped it into his pocket at the same time.

"You seem a little despondent today," she told him.

He frowned and shook his head. "Sorry. I'm just…a little distracted. Really. I'm sorry."

She smiled up at him. "You don't need to apologize. You can talk to me if something is bothering you. Is it your aunt's business? Something with your parents?" *Contessa?*

"I just…it's nothing," he sighed and then mumbled something else.

Cari thought he said *this is not how I planned it*, but that didn't make sense. "What? Not how you what?"

Bob's face registered alarm, as though he hadn't intended on voicing the words aloud. "No, it's…nothing like that. Sorry. Look, we're almost to Specter Island. We'll…"

The ferry's automatic speaker drowned out whatever else Bob said. Cari listened to the information and got ready to disembark again.

"Please wait for the ferry to be tied off before trying to step onto the pier. Please exit the ferry one at a time. We have reached Specter Island."

The message repeated three times before the tour guide spoke up. "Welcome to Specter Island. You will have one hour to explore the island instead of the fifteen minutes I gave you at our first two stops. Unfortunately, the stairs leading to the top of the lighthouse here are undergoing renovation, so you cannot climb to the top at this time. You can visit the museum inside the lighthouse to learn more about the island and the history of the lighthouse. Be sure to have your ticket stub or e-ticket available for them to scan. The ferry tour covers your cost of admission to the museum. It is currently eleven o'clock. Please be back aboard the ferry by noon."

Bob and Cari waited their turn to exit the ferry. Beyond the tall lighthouse, she could see little boutiques and restaurants as well as a bike rental shop. She wanted to read more about the history of the island, so she hooked her arm into Bob's elbow and moved him in that direction.

"Lighthouse first?" he asked her.

"Yes, I wanted to read about how the island was really named. You told me your family's story, but there has to be an older one."

"A *real* one is more like it," Bob laughed.

They made their way to the lighthouse and Bob pulled out his phone to show the attendant their e-tickets. Cari tried to steal a glance at his screen to see if he checked his texts before opening the e-tickets, but the tickets were still open on his phone from when they boarded the previous time. She groaned inwardly but painted a smile on her face.

The first exhibit had an old black-and-white photo of the island. Cari guessed it had been taken from a seaplane or other small aircraft. The caption credited a photographer and dated the photo back to 1954. She stepped closer to read the description.

Specter Island got its name from the original inhabitants of the mainland. The Native Americans who lived on the mainland thought the sound of the waves crashing into the rock wall and the caves along the shore sounded like a phantom or specter.

Cari ran her finger under the words as she read them. "Well, I guess your family's story isn't so different. This one has no mention of a buried treasure, though."

Bob laughed, "I told you. It's just a silly ghost story."

Cari started to laugh with him but stopped when she heard his phone buzz again. Rather than just a single vibration, which usually meant a text message or email, the phone continued to buzz in his pocket. He grimaced and took the phone out.

"It's my mom," he said and started to silence the call.

"Wait. You should answer it. Maybe it's something important. She knows where you are."

Bob relented and ran his thumb across the screen to answer it. "Hi, mom. Did you need something? What? Why? Okay. Fine."

He handed her the phone. "She wants to talk to you."

Cari put the phone up to her ear. "Hello, Margie? Is everything okay?"

"Everything is mostly fine. We just heard from a local reporter who is planning on running a story tonight, um, on the internet, that is, about the break-ins at The Boarding House. He wants a statement from Lydia. What is she doing to stop it? Did she notify the police? That sort of thing."

"Oh wow. I'm sure that came as a shock."

"Yes, it really knocked the wind from her sails. She's afraid an article on the internet will ruin the business. We thought you might be able to write something to paint it in the best light."

"Of course! Um, we're still on the lighthouse tour and the ferry won't start heading back for almost an hour. Did they give you a deadline?"

"Three p.m."

"We get back on the ferry at noon. I'll call you back at that point and I can dictate a statement for you or Lydia to type up."

"Thank you, Cari. Lydia says thank you too. We'll let you get back to your tour now." Margie ended the call.

Cari pulled the phone away from her ear and looked at it. "I guess she hung up."

"What's wrong?" Bob asked her.

"Your aunt is getting hounded by a local reporter—"

"Man, you really can't trust those people," Bob said with a gleam in his eye.

Cari laughed. "I know, right? Anyway, your mom thought I could put a statement together for Lydia to help The Boarding House not look, well…undesirable. Don't worry, we can still

182

finish our tour. I told her we'd call back on our return trip to the mainland."

Bob nodded, but Cari could see the disappointment in his eyes. She wondered why he wasn't thankful she was trying to help. She tried to set his mind at ease.

"Is it okay? I'm just trying to help."

Bob grabbed her hand and squeezed it. "It's great. I'm glad you can help Aunt Lydia out. Ready to finish exploring?"

* * * * *

Lydia replaced the receiver back into the phone cradle. She'd gotten three calls about the break-ins in the last hour and the news story wasn't even out yet. One was a lady from her church who heard it at the coffee shop, another was the father of one of her son Paul's childhood friends, and the most recent one hadn't identified themselves. She let out an exasperated sigh. While she hadn't tried to cover up the break-ins, she certainly wasn't advertising them either. Whoever was spreading the news wasn't very well informed either. They implied that multiple thefts had occurred and the bank was considering foreclosing on her. She balled her hands into fists.

"Was that another call about the break-ins?" Jack asked her.

She sat back in her chair. "Yes. They just keep coming. I don't know what to do."

"Keep telling them the truth. Someone broke in, but you are literally getting a security system installed today. You're working with the sheriff's office and hope the person is apprehended soon."

Before Lydia could respond, the phone rang again. Jack grabbed the receiver.

"The Boarding House. How can I help you today?"

Lydia frowned at her brother. She didn't need protecting. She could handle this.

"I'm afraid you've been misinformed. The business is not for sale…no…it's doing quite well. Yes, that's not true…yes, thank you. Goodbye." Jack hung up the receiver.

Lydia threw up her hands. "Is it ever going to stop?"

"The sheriff has the man's image. It seems nearly impossible that he doesn't live in the vicinity. He can't hide forever," Jack paused. "Not to change the subject, but have you gotten anywhere with the paperwork from the bank?"

"Not really. Between answering the phone and being available for the security system installation, I've barely looked at it." She sat up and grabbed the folder the banker had given her earlier.

"Let's look at it together." He started to drag the chair around her desk again, but picked it up and carried it when she gave him the stink eye.

"Here's the checklist. I need a six-month history of my income or profit from the bed and breakfast. What was he saying about eighteen to twenty-four months?"

"He said normally he would want more proof of income for a personal business, but because you've been a loyal customer for literally decades, he is only asking for six months."

"I guess it won't look like it's failing as badly if he doesn't see the steady decline over the last two years, but only the last six months."

"Chin up, Lyd. We're going to get through this."

* * * * *

Cari took a bite of her chicken Caesar wrap. They had grabbed an early lunch at a café near the lighthouse. She ran ideas through her head of how best to approach the guy from the newspaper. She could definitely come up with a statement to satisfy him, but she felt like Lydia needed more than that to stay ahead of the story.

"Does The Boarding House have a social media presence?" she asked Bob.

He finished chewing his bite before responding. "Uhh, it seems like it does. It definitely should, right?"

"Yes, even Ollaman got the newspaper on social media a few years ago," she said and then took another bite.

"Why do you ask?"

"I've been thinking about the news story the guy from the paper called about. It sounds like it isn't designed to be favorable for the bed and breakfast."

"I agree. Do you think you can change his mind?"

Cari frowned. "I'm not sure. I wasn't going to try, but it would be worth speaking to him. I was thinking about possibly having your aunt do something live, like on social media."

"I don't know if she'd do it. What are you thinking?"

"What if she was just completely up front? 'Someone has been breaking into my place of business, which is also my home. The local sheriff's department feels confident the same intruder is responsible for each of the break-ins. If you know anything, please come forward.'"

"I think we should probably clear that with the sheriff and her team first," Bob advised.

Cari shrugged. "It's not like we're sharing his photo or something."

"What if it spooks the guy and makes him go into hiding?" Bob challenged her.

"I don't think it will. This guy is looking for something specific. I haven't figured out what it is yet, but I think he is determined to find it. He's going to keep trying to get in until he succeeds."

Bob nodded slowly. "You might be right. I still think we should call the sheriff first."

"Fine. I'll call the sheriff. You call your aunt and pitch the idea to her," Cari agreed.

"It's a deal. One question first," Bob requested.

"What's that?"

"You said you think he's looking for something specific. Could it be the deed to the business?"

Cari thought it over before responding. "I hope your aunt doesn't have that inside the business somewhere. Did she say where the first two break-ins were?"

"He broke windows in the dining room…and helped patch one of them up with cardboard immediately after."

"Hmm…I don't think it's the deed. He would have tried to get into her office or something."

"True. Okay, I'll call Aunt Lydia. You call Sheriff Maruthers. We should probably talk and walk towards the ferry. It's getting to be close to noon," he said as he looked at his watch.

Cari nodded and gathered up her lunch trash. They tossed their garbage into the receptacle near the exit and started walking back to the ferry. She got out her phone and found the sheriff's number.

"This is Sheriff Maruthers. Ms. Turnlyle, why are you calling my cell phone?" the sheriff sounded annoyed.

"Hello, Sheriff. My apologies. I wanted to talk something through with you if you have minute."

"In the future, it would be best if you called the line for the county sheriff's office, okay?"

"Should I hang up or…?"

"No, no, you're on the phone now. Let's hear what you have to say."

"Lydia has been notified by a local reporter that he plans to run a story this evening regarding the break-ins to her business. He wants a statement from her."

Sheriff Maruthers cut in. "The media just does not quit sometimes. Man! They can get under my skin—wait, did Alex tell me you're a journalist?"

Cari bit her lip. "That's correct, Sheriff. Um, anyway. I thought maybe Lydia could get ahead of the story by doing something live on social media. Tell the viewers there have been break-ins and she needs their help to catch the guy."

The sheriff didn't respond for a few moments. Cari started to think the call had dropped when she finally spoke again. "It's a risk. Our guy Jasper-Lucien could bolt and never be caught. On the other hand, someone might have seen something or heard something. Plus, if the guy takes off, he won't be breaking in anymore, will he?"

Cari laughed. "That's true. I'm sure she would like to be confident he won't come back, though."

"Oh, agreed. You go ahead and do your live stream. Maybe I'll get Deputy Yarrow to join and see who else is watching. One more thing, Ms. Turnlyle," the sheriff requested.

"What's that?"

"In the statement she gives to the reporter, do not include the man's photo or name. If they ask, tell them to call my office."

"Will do. Thank you, sheriff."

Cari ended the call. She looked up and saw Bob was still on the phone. They had reached the pier where the ferry was tied off. Other people from their trip over were starting to arrive too. The ferry captain and tour guide were already on board but hadn't opened the walkway yet. She looked up the name of the local newspaper and found the reporter's contact info. She touched the number on the screen and confirmed she wanted to call it.

"This is Smitty with the Harborville Gazette. What's your story?" a nasally voice said into the phone.

"Hi, Smitty. My name is Cari Turnlyle. I'm a journalist too. I wanted to talk to you about a story I heard you're planning on running later today," Cari said cautiously.

"What story?"

"About The Boarding House?"

"Who told you that? Are you trying to scoop me?"

"Not at all, Smitty. I work for a newspaper in New York, but happen to be in town on vacation. I was just curious where you got the information about the break-ins."

"I have a source. Surely, you understand," he said snottily.

"Well, I'm not sure you have the whole story. You might want to wait to run it unless you want to print a correction later. Surely, you understand," she said, parroting his words.

"What are you talking about?"

"From what I've heard, it sounds like you're trying to cause trouble for The Boarding House. Wouldn't you want to support a local business instead?"

"I'm just telling the facts as I know them," he said defensively.

"And I'm trying to tell you: you don't know all the facts. Give it a day or two," she said persuasively.

"I don't know. I think the town needs to know if a place is getting broken into regularly and isn't doing anything to stop it."

"And you know that to be a fact?" she challenged.

"Uh, I, um, I contacted the business. They haven't responded yet."

"From one journalist to another, I think you should talk this over with your editor before you try to drag this business through the mud," Cari said pointedly.

"I'll keep it in mind."

The call ended. Cari looked up and saw Bob watching her.

"Well? What did Lydia think?" she asked.

"She was completely against it at first, but after I explained your reasoning *and* my mom did a little encouraging, she gave in and said she'd do it. What about the sheriff…and…was that the journalist you were just speaking with?"

"Sheriff Maruthers said no names or images of the guy we're looking for. She doesn't want that released yet. I think she is a bit concerned they won't catch him if we point him out on social media. He'll run or something. The journalist, well, I think he's at least giving the article a second thought."

The tour guide stepped up and unhooked the rope from the walkway. He motioned the passengers onboard. Bob and Cari followed the group back onto the ferry and took two seats near the front.

"I need to call your mom and help her put the statement together for the reporter. It might be better to do it before the engine starts up. It's pretty loud when we're moving."

Bob nodded and took out his phone. "Let me just unlock it and get her number pulled up for you."

Cari waited for him to pass his phone over to her then hit the call button. "Hi, Margie. It's Cari. Here's what I think we should tell the reporter…"

Chapter 14

When Bob and Cari got back to The Boarding House, Cari went straight to Lydia's office. She was hoping Margie was in there and wanted to look over the statement before it got sent to the reporter. The office door was closed, so she knocked lightly on the door.

"It's unlocked," Lydia called out from inside.

Cari opened the door and saw Bob's three relatives crowded around the computer. "What are you looking at?"

Their heads popped up in unison. Jack spoke up first. "We were just using the bank's mortgage calculator to see how the rate changes in response to different inputs. How were the lighthouses?"

Cari smiled. "They were so cool. I wish we could have gone to the top of the one on Specter Island, but the stairs are undergoing renovation. Did you know that lighthouses aren't manned anymore?"

"I think the one out in Boston still is," Margie said.

"Oh, huh. Well, none of the ones out here are. They all have digital lights. I guess robots are more reliable than people."

They laughed just as Bob walked into the office. "Do I have something in between my teeth?" he asked jokingly while baring his teeth.

"No, you look great," Cari reassured him. "Margie, or Lydia, I just wanted to look over the statement one more time before you send it off."

"Of course. Let me just pull it up," Lydia responded. She clicked the mouse a few times while Jack and Margie squeezed out from behind the desk.

"I can just turn the screen around for you to see it. I think we typed it up just as you dictated it to us," Lydia told her.

Cari scanned the words on the screen and then decided to read them aloud. "Lydia Fairchild requests the public's help regarding the break-ins to her business. The Boarding House is not only her business, but also her home. It's been her family's home for over a century and she has poured her heart and soul into it. The Boarding House is working with the county sheriff's office to apprehend the intruder. In addition, a new, state-of-the-art security system has been installed at the bed and breakfast this week. Mrs. Fairchild wants to reassure her guests and any future guests that their stay at The Boarding House will continue to be not only relaxing, but also safe."

"I think it sounds great," Margie said. "Now, when and where are we doing this live stream event? Should we make a post alerting people to it first? I sometimes see that happen in my newsfeed."

"Good idea, Mom. Why don't we say to watch for a special live video at approximately five o'clock? We can get it all planned out between now and then," Bob suggested.

"How long is this going to be?" Lydia asked cautiously. "What should I wear?"

"You should dress just as you always do. Be yourself," Cari advised. "And it's going to be short. You're just going to address the concerns of the community regarding the recent break-ins. We won't name names, but we'll say there is a person of interest and the sheriff's department is gathering information on that person as we speak. And then ask for their help. If they know anything, please call the sheriff."

"Oh! We could write the number for the sheriff's office on a notecard and hold it up at the end," Margie exclaimed.

"Perfect. Are you okay with this, Lydia?" Cari asked.

"I think so. I'd like to go over it a few times before we start. I also need to check in with my staff now that lunch is over."

Cari nodded. "Sounds good. We'll leave you to it."

* * * * *

Back in their room, Cari opened her laptop and waited for it to wake up. She thought about Genevieve's theory some more. Her friend thought everything was connected somehow and Cari was starting to agree with her.

"Brainstorming a new theory?" Bob asked her.

"Sort of. It seems highly coincidental that all of your aunt's problems started around the same time. First, the break-ins, then not long after that a realtor claims to have a buyer who wants the business, and now a reporter is stirring up trouble."

"You think someone tipped the reporter off?" Bob asked.

"Maybe. What I can't figure out is why the buyer wants the business. Genevieve suggested it was in a great location for any business, but why target this business? None of the others around here are for sale either and no one is breaking into them."

"That's probably safe to assume. I think the sheriff would have told Aunt Lydia if other businesses or homes were experiencing similar break-ins around here."

"So, it's something about this business or about your aunt. Or someone is searching for buried treasure!"

Bob laughed. "There is no treasure to search for. I mean, c'mon. You said you looked for evidence our ghost story got out and you couldn't find anything."

She grinned. "I'm going to keep digging. I don't know what I'm looking for, but I'm determined to find it," she said confidently.

Bob laughed and got out his book. He sat next to her on the sofa and started reading. Cari logged back into LexisNexis and pulled up the dry-cleaning business again. She found the pen Bob brought upstairs the day before and tapped it on the pad of paper while the information loaded.

"Hey! I just had an idea. Can you ask your aunt to let us see the offer from the realtor?"

Bob lowered his book. "Sure. I think she still has it. Why?"

"I want to give the realtor a call and find out who the interested buyer is. Maybe that's the overlap."

Bob shrugged. "I'll be right back. I'll send a text to let them know I'm coming."

He pulled out his phone as he opened the door. Cari went back to her laptop. She opened a new tab and went to a social media site. Then, she clicked back over to LexisNexis to get the employee list. She quickly jotted the names down on the paper so she could look them up on social media. She went back to the social media tab and typed 'Lucien Merrick' into the search bar. A few results popped up, but none of them resembled the man in Deputy Yarrow's photo array, and none of them lived in Minnesota or Wisconsin. She tried Jasper Benavidez next and got similar results. Looking at the employee list, she typed in the first name and found the most likely match. The person had several photos, but she didn't see anyone in them who looked like their person of interest. She crossed the name off and went to the next one.

She was on the fourth name on the list when she heard the door open. "Thank you so much," she said as she reached for the envelope.

"No problem," he said as he sat down on the sofa and picked up his book again.

Cari flipped through the contract. The realtor had said it was an anonymous buyer. She wasn't sure you could buy something anonymously, but she knew next to nothing about real estate law, so she ignored the thought. She found the realtor's phone number and punched it into her cell phone.

"Lake Shore Realty, this is Greg. How can I help you?"

"Hi, Greg. This is Cari Turnlyle. I'm calling about an offer one of your clients made on The Boarding House late last week."

"I think the offer has technically expired as it's been more than 48 hours."

Cari frowned. "Oh, well, I'm not calling to accept or decline. I *am* calling to get the buyer's name. It's not listed on the contract."

"I'm not at liberty to say," Greg responded glibly.

"Really? I mean, if the offer had been accepted, wouldn't people have found out who bought it?"

"Not necessarily. Did you have any other questions to waste my time with today?"

Cari puffed her face up in irritation. "Oh, wow. Okay. My apologies, *sir*. I appreciate your *time*." She ended the call and looked over at Bob, wondering if he noticed her frustration. He was sending a text and not paying attention. His book lay over one of his legs.

She tapped her foot, which jiggled the sofa some. The contract had to list something for the buyer. At least a business or corporation. Maybe she could find the buyer by looking into the corporation. She picked the contract up again and flipped back to the first page. The buyer was listed as another LLC: Sinclare & Associates, LLC. She looked at the list of names again and chewed on the inside of her cheek. None of the employees on the list had the name Sinclare.

She opened another tab and went to Google. She typed 'Sinclare & Associates, LLC' into the search bar and hit enter. The search engine suggested she search for *Sinclair* instead of *Sinclare*, but Cari rejected it. None of the results had anything in Wisconsin or Minnesota. Nothing looked relevant, so she went back to LexisNexis and ran the search that way. She found it rather surprising that the business did not have a website or any sort of internet presence. She supposed someone in Arizona or Florida might be wanting to buy a business up in Wisconsin, but she wasn't sure why and her gut was telling her this was something local. LexisNexis showed the LLC to have a short employee list. She quickly compared it to the other employee list, but none of the names overlapped in any way. She went to the general information section and found two associated addresses.

"No way…" she said out loud.

"What?" Bob asked, startling her.

"Sorry. I completely forgot you were sitting next to me."

He feigned hurt. "Ouch, but seriously, what did you find?"

"I looked up this business that supposedly wants to buy your aunt's bed and breakfast."

"The realtor wouldn't tell you who put in the offer?"

"I'm not even sure I talked to the realtor, but whoever *Greg* is…he wouldn't tell me anything."

Bob choked back a laugh after seeing her irritation. "Okay, so tell me what you found already!"

"The company trying to buy the business shares an address with the dry-cleaning business."

* * * * *

"Lake County Sheriff's Department, this is Deputy Yarrow speaking." The deputy's cheerful voice sounded in Cari's ear.

"Hi, Deputy Yarrow. This is Cari Turnlyle, uh, with the family of The Boarding House…" she reminded him.

"Yes, Ms. Turnlyle, I mean, Cari. We just gave Mrs. Fairchild our most recent update this morning; I'm afraid I don't have anything new to share with you."

"Oh, okay, um, I found something, actually," Cari stammered a bit.

"You found something?" Yarrow asked confusedly.

"Uh, yes. I am a journalist, so I have…never mind. I looked into the dry-cleaning business and, well, I'm not sure if you're aware, but some anonymous buyer put in an offer to buy the bed and breakfast from Lydia—"

"Okay…" Yarrow sounded even more confused.

"Right, it might not have come up, but it seemed like more than a coincidence, so I looked up the LLC behind the offer for the business and one of its addresses is the same address as the dry cleaner's."

"Uh, that…um, this puts everything in a new perspective. Hold on, let me get the sheriff in here. She's going to want to hear this too."

Cari heard a click and then static. She wasn't sure if that was better or worse than the usual on-hold music. She drummed her fingers on the coffee table while she waited. Bob had moved over to the bed and was reading his book. He must have felt her staring because he looked up and raised his eyebrows as though asking a question. She shook her head and pointed at the phone.

"Ms. Turnlyle?" the sheriff asked.

"Yes, ma'am, uh, sheriff. I'm here."

"Deputy Yarrow was just bringing me up to speed. You're telling us that the business connected to an address associated with our mystery man is also somehow connected to a business that's trying to buy the bed and breakfast…which isn't for sale?"

"That's basically what I'm saying, yes. It is a bit convoluted," she admitted.

"Okay, give us the name of the other business...now, wait a second. This is the Minnesota address, right?"

"That's correct," Cari responded.

"Well, that complicates things some," she paused. "However, we can start combing through the social media posts of those employees and maybe find our guy. Deputy Yarrow, you're young. Get on all those apps and look at their photos. If we can find our guy in one of their photos, we can figure out who we need to bring in. It might be a parent or a sibling or a girlfriend/boyfriend, but something connects our guy to this business."

"I had already started on social media. I haven't seen him yet, but I've only looked through a couple of the employee's names so far," Yarrow told her.

"I can help," Cari said, feeling a bit like she was interrupting their conversation. "I've started looking through social media already too."

"Oh! Aren't you on vacation?" the sheriff asked her.

"Well, yes, but this is what I do. I investigate," Cari told her.

"You're in law enforcement too? I thought you were a *journalist*."

Cari bit her lip before responding. "I am. I'm an investigative journalist. I've helped Alex and his partner Genevieve solve several cases back in New York."

"I thought I taught him not to like the media people. I'll have to call him..." she muttered under her breath, but Cari still heard it over the phone. "Very well, Ms. Turnlyle. Split the remaining names with my deputy. I do not want to hear about you driving over to some person's house and making some kind of citizen's arrest. Do you understand?"

Cari nodded in agreement before realizing she couldn't be seen. "I understand completely, Sheriff Maruthers. I will stick to social media searches."

"Okay, I'm going to go call the department over in Minnesota and let them know we're closing in on this guy and need their help again. Keep me posted."

Cari heard a click and thought the call might have ended when Deputy Yarrow spoke up again. "Okay, Cari. Let's get these names split up."

* * * * *

Bob slipped out of their room. He was brainstorming a new plan to propose and needed some help from Aunt Lydia and his parents. It was after three now, so they should be finished getting the statement to the news guy and possibly working on the social media update. He knew they wanted Cari to preview their take before going live. She seemed pretty engrossed in her research at the moment, so hopefully, they weren't ready for her yet. He put his ear up to the office door before knocking. He could hear them visiting, so he decided he wouldn't be interrupting a recording if he knocked.

"It's Bob," he called out as he knocked on the office door.

The door opened, revealing his mom and Aunt Lydia. "What are you up to this afternoon?" his mother asked.

"I'm scheming..." he ran his fingers through his hair. "I've been trying to find the perfect way to propose while we're here and it's like the universe is against me doing it."

"I'm sorry, honey," she glanced at the open door with concern. "Where is Cari now?"

"She's caught up in the investigation...searching social media posts of anyone linked to the dry-cleaning business."

"I thought the sheriff was doing that," Lydia asked.

Bob smiled. "Oh, the sheriff has Deputy Yarrow on it too, but Cari offered her help. Once she gets her teeth into an investigation, it is really hard to call her off."

"Okay, so what's your new plan?"

"I can already see that she's going to keep combing through social media for a photo of Lucien or Jasper or whatever his name really is until she finds him or falls asleep. So, tonight is out," he paused. "Speaking of, can we get our dinner brought upstairs again? I'm sorry to be so high maintenance."

"Of course, and you are not high maintenance!" Lydia assured him. "Just get me your orders and I'll call them into the kitchen."

"Thank you. I really appreciate it," Bob told her gratefully.

"Okay, so tomorrow is your last night here. What's the plan?" his mom needled him.

"Here's what I'm thinking, but I'm going to need some help to pull it off..."

* * * * *

Cari crossed the first name off of her part of the list. She sighed and sank back onto the couch. She tried not to be disappointed; it was never the first name on the list. Still, she had ranked the people based on their likelihood of being connected to the intruder. She figured the connection could be a sibling, parent, or girlfriend...possibly even a spouse who didn't take his name or maybe an ex-spouse.

Yarrow had split up the list alphabetically and she had ended up with the owner on her half. She felt like the owner was the least likely to be the connection as the person wouldn't have agreed to their business being associated with someone who was a criminal. Instead, she had picked Nicholas Devlin to search first. He was close in age to Lucien/Jasper, or LJ as she'd come to refer to him, assuming the age listed on Lucien's driver's license was correct.

Nicholas had most of his social media accounts set up to be private, so Cari was limited in what she could see. As a last-ditch effort, she had looked for known associates of Mr. Devlin on LexisNexis, but none of them were Lucien Merrick or Jasper Benavidez.

"And honestly, Cari, you already knew that because you looked up LJ's known associates and none of these names were on that list," she said aloud to no one as she typed the next name into the first search bar.

The doorknob turned, making her jump. "Were you talking to someone?" Bob asked her.

"Ha! You scared me. No, I was talking to myself. I feel like I'm so close to figuring out who this guy *really* is. I just need to wade through a bajillion social media posts to find him."

"Well, maybe it will cheer you up to hear I thought you might not want to quit for dinner, so I asked Aunt Lydia to have it brought up tonight."

Cari's jaw dropped. "You are too good for me, Bob Hursley. Thank you."

Bob blushed. "I'm glad I can help you out. I'd much rather arrange dinner than stare at a computer screen and look through strangers' photos for hours."

"It is pretty tedious," she admitted. "So, what's for dinner?"

"You mentioned wanting to try the rainbow trout with green beans almondine, so I put you down for that. If you want to get something else, we can call down and request a change," he added quickly.

"That sounds amazing," she bit her lip. "Any chance you ordered dessert too?"

He nodded. "Is chocolate cake okay?"

She smiled. "Chocolate cake is always okay."

"I wasn't sure when you would be hungry, so I said 6:30 for delivery."

"Perfect. Thank you so much…" she trailed off, staring at the computer screen.

"I'll let you get back to it," Bob said, but she didn't hear him. She was already back to scrolling through the images on the screen.

Deputy Yarrow had given her his cell phone number and asked her to update him as she eliminated people from her portion of the list. She picked up her phone and thumbed off a quick text that Nicholas Devlin could be taken off the list.

The next person had their accounts set to public, so Cari could see all of their information. Howard Perada was a few years younger than LJ. Cari thought he could fit the role of sibling. He had all of his photos arranged into labeled albums like "family" or "vacation" or "friends". She was surprised; most guys she knew didn't take the time to categorize their social media photos. They just uploaded them at random. She opened the family folder first. Howard was married with three young kids. Almost all of the photos were of his oldest son playing soccer. Cari scrolled through the pictures, pausing whenever a group shot came up. None of the people in the photos looked like LJ. She closed the album and went to the next one.

Her neck and shoulders felt tight from sitting in front of a laptop for the past hour. She rolled her head around in a circle and tried to relax her shoulders. Bob's phone buzzed across the room. She'd almost forgotten he was back.

"Hello? Um, let me check."

Cari looked up when she heard him speak. "What's up?"

He moved the phone away from his mouth. "Aunt Lydia says she's ready for you to preview her live social media debut. Do you have a few minutes?"

Cari hesitated. She really wanted to keep looking for the intruder, but she didn't want to let Lydia down either. "Uh, sure. Let me just mark my progress then we can head downstairs."

* * * * *

Lydia paced the room trying to calm her nerves. She wanted to appear confident and composed, not rattled and ignorant. She looked over the notecard again and tried to memorize the words.

"Sit down, woman! You are making me anxious with all that pacing," Margie barked at her.

Lydia jumped. "Sorry. I really want to get this right. Maybe I should run through it one more time."

"There is such a thing as too much practice," her brother commented.

She rolled her eyes. *There's also a thing as too much help!* "I don't want to look like a fool for all the world to see."

"For the last time, *you are not a fool!*" Jack exclaimed. "Run through it again. I suppose it can't hurt. What do I know?"

Exactly. "Okay, breathe in, breathe out...and here we go," Lydia coached herself. "Good afternoon. My name is Lydia Fairchild and I'm the owner of The Boarding House in Harborville, Wisconsin. This bed and breakfast has been in my family for over a century! It's an iconic part of our town and also my home. Recently, someone has started breaking into The Boarding House. You might hear about it...um...you might...if you watch the news...on channel...I mean...UGH!"

A knock at the door ended Lydia's stammering. Jack opened the door and ushered Cari and Bob inside. Lydia sat down in her chair and pouted.

"I'm never going to have this memorized. I sound like an idiot," she wined.

"You don't have to memorize it, Lydia. Lots of people use cue cards or a notecard. You just don't want to be looking down and reading off of it the whole time," Cari told her.

Lydia sat up. "Really? Oh, that will be so much easier. I mean, I know what I want to say. I just get three-fourths of the way through it and my mind starts getting ahead of my words and it gets completely jumbled. Can you listen to it once with me using a notecard?"

"Of course, start whenever you're ready," Cari encouraged her.

She took another deep breath and let it out. Holding her notecard up, she began again. "Good afternoon! I'm Lydia Fairchild and I'm the owner and manager of The Boarding House in Harborville, Wisconsin. This bed and breakfast was established by my ancestors over a century ago during the California Gold Rush. It's an iconic part of our town and also my home. Recently, someone has been breaking into The Boarding House. The local sheriff's office has a person of interest and is working diligently to locate the individual. I have also had a state-of-the-art security system installed—just today, in fact! In the meantime, it has frightened my guests and threatened the livelihood of my business. You might hear a news story this evening about the break-ins and The Boarding House. Please, if you know anything, contact our local sheriff's department. This is their phone number. Thank you for listening."

"That was fantastic, Lydia. You hardly looked at the notecard and did a good job maintaining eye contact. Are you ready to go outside and do it for real?" Cari asked her.

Lydia looked at her watch. It was just a few minutes before five. They'd announced their plans to go live around five in the afternoon.

"I guess it's now or never," she shrugged.

"You're going to do great. We'll be watching from inside," Margie assured her and waved her cell phone in the air.

Lydia followed Cari outside. She noticed a slight breeze lifted Cari's curls, but it felt refreshing after the stuffiness of her overcrowded office. She unlocked her cell phone and opened the social media app they'd selected for going live.

"You said something about alerting people that I was about to go live. Is that in addition to the other post saying I'd start around five?" she asked Cari.

"Yes, just say something like, 'getting set up now to go live…stay tuned' and people will see it," Cari responded.

Lydia thumbed in Cari's suggestion and clicked the 'post' button before handing her the phone. "Okay, here's my phone; I'll let you signal me when it's time to start talking."

Cari nodded. "Let me get the best angle. Stand just to your right, err, left so we can see the sign for The Boarding House behind you. Perfect. Ready?"

Cari held up the phone with both hands and mouthed *three, two, one* to her. Lydia took a breath and then smiled before speaking. She could do this.

"Good afternoon, everyone…"

* * * * *

"How many people watched Aunt Lydia's live video?" Bob asked Cari once they were back in their room.

"Well, it wasn't exactly a viral event, but the number of people increased over the course of her speech," Cari told him encouragingly.

"I hope it helps keep her in a positive light. It doesn't sound like the news article is going to," Bob said in a depressing tone. "How is your social media search going?"

"It's slow. I really thought I'd find him faster than this," she pulled out her phone to check for texts from Yarrow. "Deputy Yarrow isn't having any luck either."

"I'll let you get back to it," Bob said as he squeezed her shoulder. "Can I get you anything before I settle in to read my book?"

"I'd love some more water. Do you have any more bottles?"

"I can get you some from the kitchen. I'll be right back."

"Thank you!"

Cari unlocked her laptop and then rolled her shoulders again to ease out some of the knots. She hadn't expected to be so stressed on vacation. She had searched all but one site for Howard Perada. It was too bad there wasn't some sort of database that listed everyone's handles and usernames for every social media app out there. A lot of people didn't use their names in their handles either, which made it even harder to find them. She opened the last site and searched for a user associated with the name Howard Perada, but couldn't find one regardless of how she shortened his name.

Cari crossed him off her list. She stared at the list again before putting it back on the coffee table. Maybe she was wrong to assume the owner wasn't involved. She'd struck out so far using her theory about how LJ was connected to the business. She decided to just go back to the original list and ignore her assumptions and biases. Before she could finish typing 'Ricki Plenip' into the search bar, she heard the door to their room open.

"I have a glass of water…and…," Bob gave a dramatic pause. "Our dinner. Hope you're hungry. It looks like a lot of food."

Cari moved her laptop out of the way so Bob could put their food down on the coffee table. He had one roll of silverware stuck in each of his back pockets and was carrying a tray with two glasses of water, two glasses of wine, two salads, and two entrees. He said it down gracefully and placed all the items on the table.

"I can't believe how well you handle trays of food. I would have completely ruined dinner and probably stained my shirt if I'd tried that," Cari said admirably.

"I guess if things don't work out with the CSU, I can always go back to being a waiter," he quipped as he pulled out the rolls of silverware.

Cari accepted her utensils and placed the cloth napkin on her lap. "This looks amazing. I can't believe how great the food is here. This is possibly the best I've eaten since, well, ever!"

Cari took a bite of her rainbow trout. It was drizzled with some kind of savory sauce. If she knew anything about cooking, she might be able to name one of the ingredients. Regardless, it was delicious. The green beans were cooked perfectly too. Before she knew it, her plate was empty.

"I thought you said something about chocolate cake earlier..." she said to Bob. He was almost finished with his steak.

"Oh, right. They didn't have it plated yet. They're going to bring it up..." he looked at his watch. "Any minute now."

No sooner had he said it then someone knocked on their door. Cari jumped up. "I'll get it. Anything for chocolate."

Jack stood in the doorway holding two plates with chocolate cake drizzled with a raspberry glaze. "Bon appétit, kids."

"Thanks, Jack."

He smiled as he turned to walk away. "Any time."

Cari quickly returned to the sofa so she could try the cake. "Oh my goodness. This cake is the best. Your aunt's chef is clearly skilled."

They finished their slices of cake in silence. Cari scraped the last of the glaze off the plate with her fork and then leaned back against the back of the sofa.

"I'm stuffed," she groaned.

"Do you have time for a walk?" Bob asked with his eyebrows raised.

Cari dropped her head. "I really don't. I feel like I am so close to finding this guy. I know I keep saying that. I'm just not ready to give up yet."

Bob nodded. "I think I'll take a stroll by myself. I'll see you in a bit. Call me if you need anything."

She grabbed his hand and squeezed it before he could get away. She felt bad for not joining him, but the urge to keep looking for LJ was too strong. Just as Bob pulled the door closed behind him, her phone buzzed with an incoming call.

"Hey, Gen. How is New York?" Cari asked while she went back to typing the owner's name into the search bar.

"It's pleasant for the most part. It was a little warm over the weekend but tolerable. How are things in the Midwest? Is your headache finally gone?"

"Yes, I'm almost totally back to normal, except for some residual bruising. I'm getting better at hiding it under makeup. You almost can't tell anymore."

"That's good, I guess. Did the sheriff find the intruder yet?"

"No, but I did find a connection between the intruder and the anonymous buyer who put in an offer on the business...just like you suggested," she added.

"Awesome. What's the connection?" Genevieve asked enthusiastically.

"Well, don't get too excited. It's just the address right now. The offer came from another LLC, presumably tied to whomever the anonymous buyer is. One of the addresses associated with the LLC is the same as the dry-cleaning company the sheriff found in connection to the name Jasper Benavidez."

"Oh, interesting. So, what? Now you're scouring social media to find who is linked to Jasper, or was it Lucien?"

"I've started calling him LJ, actually," Cari chuckled.

Genevieve joined her in laughing. "Nice. Do you need any help? I don't have anything going on tonight."

Cari bit her lip as she considered her friend's offer. "I have to say no. They just barely agreed to let me help. They probably wouldn't like it if I was farming the work out to a friend, law enforcement or not."

"I understand," Genevieve told her. "Hey, how is your grandmother? I feel like I've been cut off from her with you not around all the time."

"She's doing really well. My sister was just out visiting her with her kids. I think they had a good time together, more or less," Cari responded.

"It's crazy that Bea has kids, like *big* kids. She is basically a full adult and I feel like I'm just playing pretend still. How is she doing?"

"I completely agree with that. I don't know if I'll ever feel like a real adult. But, uh, Bea's doing okay, I guess. Grandmother said she seemed upset or something about her husband's job. I'm not sure what's going on exactly."

"What company does your brother-in-law work for again?"

"Let me think. It's something with info systems…uh…New Info Systems? No, that's not it. National Technology Systems? Man. I should know this. I was just talking to Grandmother about his job earlier. Why?"

"Oh, no reason. I thought I saw an ad for New Technology Systems the other day and couldn't remember if that was his company or not," Genevieve said simply. "I should let you go. Good luck sleuthing."

"Thanks. Take care of yourself. Once I'm back, we should try to meet for dinner so you can tell me more about your training."

"It's a date. Bye, Cari."

The call ended. Cari set her phone aside and went back to searching Ricki Plenip's social media posts. The woman seemed to change her profile picture every few days, which was nice because she had all of those set to public. Cari scrolled through the posts. Occasionally, she shared posts from the dry-cleaner's social media page too. Cari tried to look at her friends list, but it wasn't set to public. She could see who liked the woman's posts, though. She started clicking through the photos and bringing up the reactions to each one.

Cari closed a photo and started to enlarge the next one, but stopped before she clicked on it. She felt like she'd already looked at over forty or fifty photos. She scrolled down the page and realized there were hundreds of photos set to public, the majority of which were profile pictures. She went back and opened the next photo. She yawned as she enlarged it.

A buzz interrupted her train of thought. She looked at her phone, but the screen was dark. She heard the buzz again a few seconds later and realized Bob had returned without her noticing. He had a serious look on his face and was responding to a text message. Her unease about Contessa drifted back into her thoughts. Was she behind all these texts? She stubbornly pushed the thought aside. She needed to focus on the photos and finding LJ. She checked the reactions to the photo and didn't see any familiar names. She closed it and opened the next one, and the next, and the next. She felt her eyes take an extra-long blink as her head bobbed up. Grabbing the glass of water, she took a drink to try to wake herself up some more. She looked back at the screen and opened another photo. Ms. Plenip was with some children at a carnival in this one. Cari wondered if they were the woman's children or nieces/nephews.

"C'mon, Cari. Your head has almost hit the computer screen four times now. You shouldn't overdo it this soon after getting a concussion. Let's go to bed."

Her head snapped up and she opened her eyes. "I didn't realize how tired I am. You're right. The photos will still be here tomorrow. Let me just text Yarrow and tell him I'm calling it a night."

"I think he already texted you. Your phone buzzed like three times a minute or two ago," Bob informed her sleepily.

Cari gave him a sheepish grin. "Sorry. I completely lost track of time. I'm going to brush my teeth."

"Be fast. I'm tired too," Bob groaned from the bed.

Chapter 15

Cari woke up to the sunshine peeking into their room from behind the curtains. Bob was already out of bed. She looked towards the bathroom and heard the shower running. She mentally debated about trying to get some more sleep or going back to the photos from the previous night. In her dreams, she had been clicking through the photos again, but she couldn't get them to come into focus. Everything was blurry, almost like she was looking at them through a distorting lens. She threw back the covers and walked barefoot over to the sofa.

Her laptop was still open from the previous night. She ran a finger over the mouse pad to wake it up and logged in. The photos were still up on the screen. She had left the last one open. She double-checked the reactions, but didn't find a familiar name. She sighed and moved on to the next photo. Staring back at her was the man from the photo array.

"Now I've got you, LJ," she said, pointing at the screen.

"Who's LJ?" Bob asked from the bathroom doorway, a towel wrapped around his waist.

"Oh, goodness! You startled me. Um, LJ is my personal nickname for the intruder. Rather than say or write Lucien-Jasper, I just call him LJ for short."

"Ah, and it sounds like you found him?"

"Well, I definitely found a photo of him with the owner of the dry-cleaners," she responded. "It's on her social media. I'm going to check the reactions and see if he's on the list."

"And call Deputy Yarrow to give him an update?"

Cari grinned at Bob. "And that too. Yes." She pumped her fist in the air. "He didn't react to the photo—maybe he isn't on social media at all, but his *sister* put a caption on the photo: *celebrating the return of my brother, George.* It's from this year. It's definitely him. I'm going to take a screenshot…and then call Yarrow."

She pressed the screenshot button with her left hand and grabbed her phone with her right. She hadn't plugged her phone in last night and it was really low on battery. She unlocked the screen and saw her text thread with Yarrow was still open. She hit the call symbol and waited for him to answer.

"Deputy Yarrow speaking," a drowsy voice said over the line.

"I found him!" Cari almost shouted into the phone.

"Wait, what? That's amazing. I'm so tired of looking at all these photos; plus, we've been getting calls on and off from people who claim to know about the break-ins, but actually know nothing," he sighed. "Where is he?"

"Oh, I only found him on social media. Well, on his sister's social media. The owner of the dry-cleaning business has a photo of him and the caption refers to him as her brother…George." Cari reported proudly.

"Send me a copy. This should get the guys over in Minnesota interested, at least enough to go pick her up. Hopefully, she'll talk and tell us where *George* is. Good job, Ms. Turnlyle…" he paused. "Wait, did you say brother? I don't have a record of Ms. Plenip having a brother."

"I don't know what to tell you. That's what the caption says," Cari responded.

"Well, good work, Ms. Turnlyle."

"Cari. And thanks," she told him.

"I'm going to talk to the sheriff. She'll get the department in Minnesota to help us out. This could all be wrapped up by the end of the day if we're lucky."

The call ended. Cari went back to the photo and looked at the list of people who reacted to it again. It seemed likely LJ wasn't using either alias on social media, but maybe he was on there under a different name. There were no Luciens, Merricks, Jaspers, or Benavidezes on the list. She looked for a George on the list, but didn't see one.

"Did you lose him?" Bob asked, startling her again.

Cari shook her head. "No, I was just looking for someone named George who reacted to the photo, but none of them are."

"Well, I mean, he's done a fairly okay job of covering his tracks so far, right? He's not going to risk someone making that connection so easily."

"True. I wonder if she's friends with someone named George. Maybe I can find him on here."

She went back to the woman's friend list and started to search for *George* when Bob put his hand on the edge of the screen. She looked up at him with her eyebrows raised.

"Maybe you could look for him after breakfast?" he asked quietly.

She drew her lips into her mouth and took a breath. "Of course. You're right. We're on vacation and I gave the information to Deputy Yarrow. I'll get in the shower and be ready before you know it."

* * * * *

Cari stared out the window at Lake Superior while she chewed a bite of her omelet. Sailboats dotted the horizon and seagulls were swooping near the surface in search of fish. She wondered if the Coast Guard had been able to locate the driver of the speedboat that nearly capsized them a few days ago. Her bruises were almost gone now, but the experience was still fresh. She was disappointed they hadn't gotten to return to the cave. They had been so close when the guy shot past them. It almost seemed intentional, like he was trying to prevent them from getting to the cave, but why would anyone care about that? She heard Bob clear his throat and shifted her gaze back to him.

"I'm sorry, did you ask me something?"

He looked her in the eyes before responding and sighed. "I was mentioning some ideas of how we could spend our last day here. Did any of them sound fun?"

She winced. "I'm sorry. I was off in my own world. I didn't hear any of what you said."

He blinked and then spoke again. "There's a museum in town, uh walking distance from here. It gives some of the history of the area. We could go on a hike. There are trails which take you right along the lake. Some of them lead down to the beach and you can go swimming. I'll warn you though, it's pretty cold even though it's summertime. I'm guessing you don't want to go kayaking again."

Cari smiled. "I won't rule out kayaking on a future trip, but I don't think I'm ready to do it again this time. The hike sounds like fun. How long is it?"

"We can make it however long or short we want. First, we take the car onto a ferry and ride it over to one of the islands nearby. There's a state park and it has several trails to choose from. Some are loops and some are out and back type hikes," he explained.

"Let's do a hike. Maybe we can bring our swimsuits and decide if we want to swim after testing the temperature of the water with our feet," she suggested.

"Works for me. Is there anything else you'd like to do on our last day here?"

214

"Besides catch the criminal that's been breaking into the building?" she asked, clenching her right hand.

Bob grimaced. "Hopefully, the sheriff's department has that under control. I don't think there's much more you can do, right?"

She sighed. "I suppose not."

"Are you finished eating? I need to buy a ferry ticket before we leave."

"I can run upstairs and get our swimsuits while you do that. Is the sunscreen still in your backpack?"

"We can go up together. I want to brush my teeth before we head out."

Bob signaled the waitress for their bill. She pulled it from her apron pocket and brought it over.

"Can I get you anything else? Coffee refill or coffee to go?" she asked.

Bob looked at Cari before responding. She shook her head no. "I think we're all set. Thanks."

He entered their room information onto the paper and returned it to the little book. Cari wondered how much the trip had cost so far. He hadn't let her pay for anything yet, though, to be fair, she realized she hadn't really offered either. She bit her lip, feeling a little ashamed.

"Um, I feel silly just bringing this up now. I haven't paid for anything this week...I haven't even *offered* to pay for anything. Everything has been amazing, but it must be costing you a fortune."

Bob's face reddened. "Um, I'm getting the uh, *family rate* here. This is something I wanted to do *for* you. I had a ton of frequent flyer miles saved up on my credit card and used those for our flights. Don't sweat it. I'm glad we've gotten to spend a week together. I've had fun too. Ready to get our hiking stuff together?"

She grinned and stood up. "I'm right behind you."

They climbed the steps back to their room. Bob unlocked the door and went straight for the bathroom. She crossed the room to the dresser and fished around in the drawers for her swimsuit. She hadn't seen it since she unpacked last Wednesday but knew it had to be in there somewhere.

"I'm just going to brush my teeth, then I'll get the sunscreen and everything packed up," Bob called out from the bathroom.

Cari found her swimsuit and set it on the bed. She got out her phone and checked to see if she had missed any texts from Deputy Yarrow. Nothing. Her laptop was still open on the coffee table. She heard Bob running the water in the bathroom and stood up to look for the mystery man's name again. The water stopped and she froze and turned towards the bathroom instead. Bob was right. She'd done what she could; it was time to let the sheriff handle it now. She looked at her phone's screen again, but no messages appeared.

"Is everything okay?" Bob asked as he came out of the bathroom.

She glanced up. "It's fine. I was just, uh, checking to see if Yarrow had sent me an update on the case...but now, I am putting my phone in my pocket. I'll only take it out for photos. No more sleuthing...unless I'm asked."

He laughed. "I'm going to hold you to that."

* * * * *

Lydia drummed her fingers on her desk and then clicked the refresh button again. Normally, the bed and breakfast's rooms were reserved a few months in advance. It was slower in the winter months, but they still had guests who came hoping to try their hand at ice fishing, ice skating, or even snowshoeing. October was less than four months away and the calendar only had a handful of reservations. She sighed and closed the window. Much like a watched pot, the calendar wasn't going to boil over with reservations while she sat and stared at it.

It was getting close to the end of the lunch shift already. She'd spent the morning filling out the rest of the paperwork for the bank and gathering the necessary documents. She and Jack had an appointment later in the week to hopefully get the refinancing finalized. She needed to go check with the housekeeping staff since two of the rooms checked out that morning. Her phone rang before she could get out of the office.

"The Boarding House. This is Lydia. How can I help you?"

"Lydia. It's Sheriff Maruthers. I have some good news. Do you have a minute?"

Lydia sat back down in her chair. "Of course. You said good news, so I always have time for that."

The sheriff laughed. "Well, I'm glad to hear that. I have quite the tale to share with you. Deputy Yarrow, with the help of your Ms. Turnlyle, found a connection to the dry-cleaning business and the person who tried to buy your business. Since the dry cleaner is over in Minnesota, we had to coordinate with the folks over there, but they went by and picked up the owner."

"Right. The kids mentioned something at breakfast about her having a photo of her brother on social media…and the brother looking basically identical to Jasper or whatever his name is," Lydia interjected.

"Correct. They picked up the owner this morning and let Deputy Yarrow sit in while they questioned her. At first, she pretended not to know anything about anything. She doesn't know a Lucien Merrick or anyone named Jasper. We had her photo of her brother with the caption saying it was her brother and the evidence of her business being associated with one of his aliases. When she saw that, she changed her tune. Now this is where it gets interesting.

217

"Apparently, her brother—his real name is George Sinclare, by the way—is something of a recreational treasure hunter. Also, he's not really her brother. They were childhood friends who have stayed close through the years and consider each other family. She occasionally loans him money. About a year ago, he bought this old chest at a garage sale somewhere. The chest had a secret compartment—"

"You're kidding me!" Lydia exclaimed.

"No, I am not. It had a compartment and inside, he found an old diary. He skimmed the entries and one of them mentioned a trip out to your bed and breakfast! The diary's owner overheard some tall tale about a gold miner hiding his treasure out in a cave along the lake—"

"Oh no. Not the ghost story…" Lydia whispered.

"You've heard this story? It's *real*?" Sheriff Maruthers questioned her.

Lydia let out a nervous laugh. "I don't think it's real at all. It's just this story that my grandfather passed down to his son—my father, and my father told it to his grandkids. If my kids give me grandkids, I'll probably tell it to them too. But it's not true. It's just a silly family story. Folklore that we tell the youngest generation at family gatherings, but there was never any truth to it."

"Well, I for one am relieved I don't have to retell that whole story to you," she laughed. "Anyway, this man thought the story was true and he's been out here for a couple months searching for the treasure *and* the treasure map."

"He confessed? You found him?" Lydia asked with hopefulness.

"We found him and he confessed to the break-ins. We have him dead to rights on those. There was no reason for his palm print to be up on the balcony railing and he knew it. He is also responsible for the kayaking accident last week too," the sheriff informed her.

218

"I can't believe she was right; I mean I can, but wow." Lydia said in amazement.

"What do you mean?"

"Bob, my nephew, he told me Cari thought this intruder must have heard our little story and came out here to dig for treasure. But how does a recreational treasure hunter afford a speedboat? And the LLC behind the anonymous buyer? You said that was him too? If he's out searching for treasure all day, how does he have any money?"

"You met him. He's very charismatic. I haven't gotten to the end of his list of crimes, but I'm going to guess he has swindled some investors into funding his treasure hunting habit. He has managed to create two aliases that have very legitimate looking identification," she explained. "As far as compensation to you and your business…it might take a while. But at least you can honestly tell people the intruder has been captured. Who knows? Maybe the ghost story will bring you some business too."

"As long as they aren't trying to tear the wallpaper off the walls, I'll be happy to have them."

* * * * *

Cari put down her window to let the fresh air into the car. She hadn't ridden on a ferry like this in years and had forgotten how relaxing it could be. The seagulls were lined up along the piers to her right. She imagined they were watching the surface for a fish to catch. She felt her phone vibrate with an incoming call. The number looked familiar, but she couldn't place it.

"Hello? This is Cari. Who's this?"

A vaguely familiar nasally voice responded. "It's Smitty…you know, with the newspaper. You called me about my article?"

She nodded, remembering him from yesterday. "I completely forgot to check. Did you end up running it?"

"Thankfully, no. I really thought you were trying to scoop me or something, but my boss looked you up and showed me you weren't lying about working in New York…" he paused and Cari waited for him to continue. She looked over at Bob and mouthed *reporter guy* to him. He started to nod when his own phone buzzed with an incoming call. Cari turned back to the window when Smitty started talking again.

"Anyway, I guess I'm calling to say thank you for warning me about the story. We just heard from the sheriff's department that they caught the guy—"

"Wait, what?!" Cari and Bob exclaimed in unison, startling each other. Cari looked at him with wide eyes and Bob gave her a thumbs up.

"They caught the intruder! I thought you would know. They told me you helped track him down."

"Uh, I did a little, I guess," she said humbly. "I hadn't heard yet that they caught him, though."

"Well, they did. They called me because…well, I guess I almost got duped by him too," he said shamefully.

"What do you mean?"

"This guy called me the other day. He told me he had a story about a local business trying to cover up break-ins to keep from losing business. It sounded pretty shady on the owner's part. The guy knew a lot about it too…like the dates of the break-ins and stuff. I checked our scanner history and it all matched up."

"Okay, but that doesn't sound like you were duped. It was just a source giving you a story," Cari pressed him.

"Yeah, well, he told me if I ran the story, I would get a reward."

"A reward for what?" Cari asked, dumbfounded.

"I don't know. I just heard reward and decided it was mine. It turns out, he was the guy breaking in. He was just trying to scare that lady into giving up her business so he could go on a stupid treasure hunt. Can you believe that?"

"After the week I've had, I could believe almost anything."

* * * * *

When they got back to The Boarding House, Lydia greeted them at the front door. She was grinning from ear to ear. Cari smiled back. She knew it must be a relief to have the intruder, or George Sinclare, off the streets at last.

"Bob, Cari! We're having a little celebration tonight. You're eating at the restaurant, right?" she asked earnestly.

Bob nodded. "Of course, Aunt Lydia. It's our last night here. We'll be there."

They made their way up to their room. Cari slipped out of her sneakers and set them aside. Dinner was in less than two hours, so she needed to wash the sweat and grime away.

"I'm going to get in the shower again," she told Bob. "I take it we should dress up tonight?"

Bob nodded. "I think Aunt Lydia is hoping for a bit of a party. It was great to see her so relaxed just now, huh? She's been really tense."

Bob's phone buzzed before Cari could respond. He pulled it out and read the message. She waited for him to say something, but he looked surprised when he realized she was watching and slipped the phone back into his pocket.

"I'll be fast so you have time to shower and get ready too," she told him.

Luckily, she hadn't washed her hair earlier, so it wouldn't get dried out from washing it now. She grabbed her dinner attire and set to work on getting cleaned up. They had climbed up and over several boulders along the lake shore during their hike and she had some mud crusted onto her right calf. The shower felt great and somehow her hair wasn't horribly difficult to get her pick through when she got out. Rather than take the time to dry her hair, she pulled it back into a loose bun and let some of her curls fall out to frame her face. She pulled on her sundress and then grabbed her makeup supplies to take into the room.

Bob was on his phone again when she stepped into the room. She cleared her throat to get his attention. He jumped and almost dropped his phone.

"Oh, you're out. I, uh, I wasn't paying attention. Uh, you look nice," he stammered. "I'll get in the shower now. See you in a bit."

She sat down in front of the mirror in their room and started applying her makeup to hide what remained of the bruises on her face. When she was done, she grabbed her phone to take a selfie. She sent it to Genevieve and Grandmother.

One last night in Wisconsin

Genevieve responded first: Don't you clean up nice

Her grandmother called instead of responding with a text.

"Hi, Grandmother!"

"You look lovely my dear. I can't even tell that your face is bruised anymore. I can see the stitches still. Will they have to take those out at some point?"

"Thank you! They told me they would dissolve when the cut heals."

"Your last night of vacation, huh? What does Mr. Bob have planned?"

"Well, his aunt is having a little celebration because they caught the guy!"

"The intruder! That's wonderful news. She must be so relieved."

"I think she is. I only just met her, but she seems much more at ease now," Cari agreed.

The bathroom door opened and Bob stepped out wearing black pants and a bright blue polo. Cari raised her eyebrows at him. She wasn't sure she'd ever seen him wear a shirt that bright before or pants that were anything other than khaki.

"Well, I'll have to tell you all about how they caught the intruder later, Grandmother. It's almost time for us to go down for dinner. Good to chat with you. Love you!"

"I love you more, dear. Have fun."

* * * * *

The dining room was the fullest Cari had seen it since they'd arrived at The Boarding House. Every table was filled and it seemed like there were extra waitstaff on hand too. She was surprised that Bob's parents hadn't sat with them but was glad they got the table in the corner one last time. It had the best view of the lake.

She had ordered filet mignon for dinner. It was the first time she hadn't eaten one of the fish entrees since they'd gotten to Wisconsin. The steak was perfectly cooked and came with asparagus and garlic mashed potatoes. She looked at Bob, who was pushing a forkful of fish around his plate. His forehead had a sheen of perspiration on it. She started to ask him if he was okay when his phone buzzed with another text. She almost rolled her eyes, but looked out the window instead. It was so unlike him to be on his phone this much. She had thought he was caught up worrying about his aunt's business, but that seemed to have worked itself out. Yet, here he was on his phone again. Not that she was any better, she reminded herself. She had ignored him half of yesterday and part of this morning, trying to chase down the intruder.

She sighed. He was probably getting tired of always being second to whatever story she was investigating. Even on their vacation, she had put her sleuthing ahead of him; no wonder he was paying so much attention to his phone. She started to turn back to him when she heard a clink against some glassware. Lydia's voice rang out over the dining room conversations.

"Hello, everyone! If I could just have a moment of your time. The waitstaff will be coming around to clear your dinner dishes, then we have a complimentary dessert—on the house—" she paused while everyone cheered. "I want to thank all of you for being here tonight. We've had a rough month or so here at The Boarding House, but today we finally got some good news. They found the man who was breaking in here and apprehended him. And it's in part thanks to my new friend, my dear nephew's *girlfriend*, Cari Turnlyle."

Cari felt herself blushing but tried to smile naturally at everyone when they turned to look her way.

"She and my nephew, Bob, were instrumental in helping to track down this criminal and put a stop to his activities," Lydia paused again when she saw the waitstaff returning with trays of champagne. "And now, if you will all join me in a champagne toast—"

Cari started to look at Bob out of the corner of her eye, but he was gone. She looked over to the hallway that led to the restrooms, thinking he must have slipped off that way, but he wasn't there. She realized Lydia was no longer speaking and felt everyone's eyes on her. Bob cleared his throat, drawing her eyes down to where he was kneeling on the floor in front of her seat.

"Cari, this last week has been nothing like I imagined it would be. You startled an intruder, you almost died while kayaking, you helped my aunt save her business. I know...I know you always say," he gulped as a tear streamed down his face. "I know you always say I'm too good for you, but that isn't true. You are everything to me and I'm so glad we're together. Caroline Turnlyle, will you marry me?"

The End

Did you enjoy the book? Please leave a review!

224

Don't worry, Cari has more stories to write! Stay tuned for Book 5: The city of Brenington is shocked to learn that one of its residents is actually best-selling author Natasha Gillespie. Just days after announcing her retirement and revealing her identity to the world, Gayle Smith, i.e., Natasha Gillespie, is found dead in her own home. Cari is not alone in suspecting foul play; Genevieve and Alex lead the investigation after barbiturates are discovered in the woman's system. The three must work alongside each other once again to find the murderer.

Visit https://leslieapiggott.com for more information and to join my e-newsletter list.

A Note from the Author

"The Mystery of Specter Island" was inspired by a trip my husband planned for us in 2022. We visited the town of Bayfield, Wisconsin, which is also right on the coast of Lake Superior. Bayfield is home to The Old Rittenhouse Inn, which has many similarities to the fictitious bnb you read about in the book. The story of Bob and Cari going for a run together is based on a true story of my husband and I running up the hills in Bayfield. Much like Bob, Brad planned the entire trip, including a kayaking trip. Ours was a group trip, but we did get to kayak inside a couple of caves, which is where the image on the cover of the book was taken. I changed the name of "Devil's Island" to "Specter Island" to avoid offending anyone local to the area as well as giving me the liberty to create my own folklore about the place. If you've never visited Wisconsin or Lake Superior before, I highly recommend it. We had a wonderful time!

Acknowledgments

Thank you to my dear friend, Desiree, for letting me bounce ideas off of her for the book and for always reading the draft. Your assistance is invaluable!

As always, a big thank you to my editor, Jennie Rosenblum for her amazing work in polishing my writing.

Congratulations to Dale McClure for winning my contest and getting a character in the book this time. I hope you enjoyed the experience!

And finally, to all of my readers: thank you for your dedication and support.

About the Author

Leslie A. Piggott lives in the Austin, Texas area with her husband and their two children. She is a scientist-turned-mom who received her doctorate in Biomedical Sciences from the University of Texas Health Science Center at Houston. In addition to writing, she also enjoys running marathons, quilting, knitting, singing in the church choir, and watercolor painting. She has previously published two watercolor and poetry books, both in 2021: *Poems in the Pandemic*, and *Art in Words*. Her first novel, *Rising Pressure* was published in January of 2022. To sign up for her e-newsletter, you can visit her website at https://leslieapiggott.com.

Printed in the USA
CPSIA information can be obtained
at www.ICGtesting.com
CBHW011400211223
2832CB00010B/110